PLAY
THE
DEVIL

---

a novel

Scott Laudati

.Bone Machine, Inc.

Final Edition

ISBN: 0-578-73683-7
ISBN-13: 978-0-578-73683-9

BONE MACHINE, INC.
14 Allen Avenue
Manasquan, NJ 08736

Copyright © 2021, Scott Laudati
ReadBoneMachine@gmail.com

Edited by: Maura Power & Glen Binger
Cover by: Carlos Gonzalez-Fernandez
Logo by: Drew Alexander Ennis

Printed in the United States of America

also by SCOTT LAUDATI

.poems.

Hawaiian Shirts In The Electric Chair
Bone House
Camp Winapooka

DEDICATION

Joey Belasco, a better friend than I could've asked for.

Edward Thorn, the master story teller, my most important educator.

Ronald Ennis, for feeding me jellyfish and showing me the world.

Ben Matulich, for always being cool and never being a moron.

BASED ON A TRUE STORY

Play The Devil

CHAPTER ONE

1

Let me tell you about being a hero.

I had just crossed halfway through my twenty-fourth year, a snakebit milestone, the age of James Dean dead. I was staring at the ceiling of my college dorm with lapsarian apathy, excited about nothing. It left me feeling like the last outlaw. I was on the verge of a very important night: the night I decided to quit for good.

It was a foul hour in early May, and I had been sitting in lotus position long enough for both of my legs to go numb. The war was playing on TV, and I was looking for any reason not to call my parents and explain my decision to take another sabbatical. Three years had passed since I'd last quit college. It seemed like the right time to walk away again.

I hadn't slept in days and the Adderall I'd bought from the girl who charged $100 to write my paper on Upton Sinclair didn't seem to be wearing off. I got up and walked to the student center, but I forgot to bring my ID and couldn't rent a pool cue.

I walked back to my dorm.

There wasn't much to do so I began thinking. I looked around my room. I counted ten dirty cups of coffee and six Moleskine notebooks. The coffee cups depressed me. Each one promised a clean morning: drink a cup of black coffee and begin writing the next great American novel.

But the novel never got written.

Each cup reminded me I had one less day to prove that I mattered.

The Moleskines lay around my bed in anticipation of a midnight flash that refused to come. Their covers were stained with old coffee rings. The insides hadn't fared any better. Most of the pages were filled with drawings of the animals humping out in the quad.

Spring was in bloom and I was the only thing not getting laid.

I considered sitting on the floor and doing some sit ups, but it seemed like a dumb time to start improving. No prospects. About to be a third-time college dropout. A loser to everyone but the family dog. No amount of sit ups was going to help me.

I went to brush my teeth instead.

I stared at myself in the bathroom mirror for a long time. Trying to understand why life was always like this. Eventually I gave up, and when I looked away I saw the Upton Sinclair book my teacher had assigned, *The Jungle*, sitting next to the toilet tank. It must've belonged to my roommate. We'd been friends for about a week and then he pledged a frat. He promised to "hook up" his "boy" at their parties but I barely ever saw him again.

I picked up the book and thought about our last conversation: "They made us do an elephant walk," he'd said about his frat brothers. "It actually wasn't that bad."

I flipped to the first chapter with the toothbrush in

my mouth. On page twenty, tears started dropping from my eyes. I brushed until the bristles were red. Then I went back to my room and threw all my textbooks into the garbage can.

It took three boxes to empty my dorm. I buried the Moleskines at the bottom. My mother had bought them for me after I'd told her I wanted to be a writer. All I'd done in that time was write one short story everyone hated.

Even my mother.

I walked to my car and packed the three boxes into the trunk. Then I headed to the library to find an unabridged copy of *The Jungle*.

I read for nine straight hours. Around noon the next day I drank coffee. I reread the last line of *The Jungle* - "CHICAGO WILL BE OURS!" - and closed the book.

In the computer lab I Googled: *The American Dream*. The definition was just another ethos, one of those "all men are created equal," or "give us your tired, your hungry," or whatever. I didn't buy it. It relied too much on everyone playing by the rules.

I felt dead. Like my parents were dead. Like all the drooling dogs on earth were dead. I walked outside and watched the girls' track team circle the lake. I thought of Holland and the spring tulips that were probably just starting to bloom. I thought of renting a bicycle and riding it to California.

2

The admissions building sat on a hill like an old Masonic temple. I climbed the steep road that led to its front doors and passed the last American chestnut tree. It was our school mascot. I looked at the initials couples had carved into its old bark. Maybe all that love is what's keeping the tree alive, I thought.

I smoked a cigarette on the steps of the admissions building. The biggest American flag I've ever seen was flying perfectly horizontal over the roof. Not a crease. The blue sky behind it looked like freedom. I thought about the last line of *The Jungle*. If Chicago could beat *the man*, so could I.

I turned my fist out and held it up to the flag. Then I went inside.

An old lady wearing two hearing aids and a pantsuit saw me in the hallway and called me into her office. I declared my intentions and she put together a folder of withdrawal papers.

"Is Londi your first name or last?" she asked.

"First."

She clicked something on her computer and then slid the folder over to me. A bowl full of cheap sunglasses sat on her desk with our school's name printed on them. I picked one out and put it on and asked her if she wanted to know why I was quitting.

She didn't look up. "No."

I signed at the top and bottom of the last page and gave the folder back.

"Good luck," she said.

Tables were set up in the hallway for club recruitment. History Club. Campus Christians. Greek Life. Federalist Society. Naked Singularity. Vegan Easter. An entire world existed that I'd never noticed.

A bald girl at the Philosophy and Fight Club table handed me a yellow button with purple writing. I studied it while leaving the building. It said:

Are You A Victim Of Adolescence?

Outside, I brought my eyes up from the button to the flag. Something had changed. It had all changed. A strong wind blew, but now the flag hung like a deflated balloon. The blue sky had been eaten by gray clouds. It looked like a hurricane was rolling in.

I pinned the button onto my chest.

In my car I put on a Bright Eyes record that sounded like snow and country roads. Then I drove to happy hour at the bar around the corner.

I drank for a long time. I imagined the Norman Rockwell scene of my family back at home getting ready to eat dinner. Around the fourth pint I gained some confidence. I texted my mother: *I quit. I'm a victim of adolescence.*

That seemed right. I finished my beer and got a text from my father as I was paying up: *Don't come home without a job.*

"How serious do you think he is?" I asked the bartender.

"If you were my son I'd already have your room rented out."

I ordered a shot and downed it and then walked to my car. I rested my head against the steering wheel and listened to Bright Eyes for a while. A police car was parked a few spots down. Exhaust steamed out from the tailpipe. The engine hummed. I pictured the fat face of the cop, sweaty and aroused, just waiting for me to chance driving. For me to give him an excuse.

It was dark but I put my sunglasses on. I lit a cigarette. On my way passed the cop I yawned and stuck a finger in my nose.

3

I stopped at a Home Depot about a mile from my parents' house. I'd been seeing commercials for their new garden center all month. My mother liked things like that. I thought a purple orchid might be the peace offering she'd need to stay on my side.

The Home Depot lights lit up the parking lot like a stadium. Every bug in the state was buzzing around the plastic glow. Huge bats swooped through like a school of hungry bluefish. I watched the bats dive down and miss people's heads by inches, but nobody noticed. Even the cart boy had his eyes locked on a phone.

What have we become, I thought? We could've done anything, and this is what we did.

I parked next to a truck with an attached horse trailer. It had West Virginia plates. A horse with a black head and black mane stuck most of its head out of the trailer window and looked at me.

"I'll bet you're happy to be in New Jersey," I said.

The horse did a move with its mouth that looked like a smile. I stopped to pet its head and scratch its chin for a while. Then I went inside.

I had to maze through aisles of lumber and toilet appliances until I hit the garden section. Everything was dry and brown and covered in a thick dust. I found an orchid that looked half-alive and headed toward the register.

A crowd was gathering around the customer service desk. I heard a familiar voice growing louder and angrier: "What do you mean I can't buy muriatic acid? I'm a licensed pool boy!"

It was Frankie Gunnz, my best friend since the HYAL basketball days. He pulled off his shirt like he always did before a fight. It let everyone see the faded Italian flag tattooed between his shoulder blades. Which was usually all it took to end a fight before it started.

"Frankie," I said. "What's going on?"

The crowd parted for me when I started speaking. Frankie turned around and seemed a little less angry when he realized it was me. "Londi, listen to this one. These Home Depot mutts think they've got me on my back."

A fascist with a manager tag banged a clipboard against the desk. "Muriatic acid is on the Attorney General's List. It is banned. What do you want from me?"

"Do I look like a terrorist?" Frankie said to the crowd. "When the nursery was in business, I could buy buckets of chemicals."

A collective "boo" came from the herd of onlookers.

"Are you ready to lose two customers?" I asked the manager.

He called my bluff. I bought the flower.

Frankie and I walked to my car. A man and woman with matching cowboy hats were sitting in the truck with the horse.

"I bought three buckets of muriatic acid here last week," Frankie said.

"They'll put us all in camps soon," I sighed.

"My parents hate grass so I've been spraying it all over their yard. But the grass just keeps growing."

"You surrounded your parents' house with muriatic acid? If the wind kicks up you'll kill the neighbors."

"Apparently it's not *that* dangerous. It can't even kill grass."

The cowboy started making growling sounds. We turned around to see what was wrong. His wife was in the driver's seat. He leaned over her and stuck his head out the window. Looked strangely like his horse. "How is my horse supposed to get any sleep with you two making so much noise?"

"Take it to a horse hotel," Frankie said to him.

"Another goddamn Jersey WOP. You think you can just hang out in parking lots and talk shit?"

The cowboy's wife chewed on a hamburger and shook her head at us.

"With a face like that, I'd put your wife in the trailer and keep the horse up front," Frankie said.

The cowboy's head started to hemorrhage in a fit. "In front of my wife? You talk like this in front of my wife?" He grabbed the hamburger from his wife's mouth and pulled his hand back to throw it at us. The hamburger hit the window visor and exploded all over her face. A pickle slid down her chin.

"I can't see," she cried. "There's barbecue sauce in my eyes."

"Look what you made me do to my wife." He pointed at the orchid I was holding. "I'm going to stick that flower up your asshole!"

He opened his door but got caught in his seatbelt. He yanked at it a few times before he gave up.

"Every time I come to New Jersey ..." he said.

4

I drove Frankie to his car on the other side of the parking lot.

"How long are you in town for?" he asked.

"Indefinitely."

"Pool season is starting up. Call me if you need a job."

5

I stopped to buy a case of Portuguese beer and then went home. I found a free version of *The Jungle* online and reread most of it. I'd always known we were doomed, but now I had it in writing. I can finally say school was good for something, I thought.

The only thing left to do was join the Socialist party, but I wasn't sure if that was even legal. I drank the beer and thought about everything on earth. When the beer was done I smoked cigarettes and watched Kurosawa films on TV until dawn guilted me to bed.

CHAPTER TWO

I never liked pools.

The summer came late, as it always did in New Jersey. Just after another winter retreated and left us with a day or two of spring. And I would spend them with my old man getting bitched around our backyard, dragging filter cartridges and ladders from the shed to the pool while the birds watched the reopening of their favorite bath.

I never even used the thing.

My mother wouldn't have it any other way. The pool had to be opened before Memorial Day. It had to be the father-son episode we avoided all year. She was concerned we didn't do enough together.

It was the concept of a pool that I couldn't make sense of. What a thing, I thought. A human pond filled with water that was always too cold. All my sweaty friends and dirty little cousins hopped right in; piss and parasites swimming around while everyone relaxed on inflatable alligators.

Once the pool was opened I could avoid the hair clots and dead spiders for the rest of the season. But eventually the nights grew longer. The air smelled like nostalgia. I knew the fat lady would be singing soon.

And so came that fateful day in early fall when the pool needed to be closed. As quickly as those friends and cousins came over and swam, they all managed to disappear just before work time.

Like a prison alarm clock my father would pound on my door with a Hard Knock proverb: "You can't howl with the hogs if you want to soar with the eagles." So I'd wake up, go to the backyard, and find a pool cover that smelled like it had been dragged through a New York City subway tunnel. A heap in the grass covered in mouse turds. Bird feathers. Ants.

A heavy sweat fell while I pulled the cover around the foundation. Goosebumps rose when I had to stick a limb in the water and plug the pressure drained lines.

Motivation is difficult to find when the end result is something you never wanted in the first place.

CHAPTER THREE

1

I woke up and wondered if my old friends had moved on without me. I was in that strange period men hit in their mid-twenties when the fork in the road can't be avoided any longer. Some go on, climb the ladder, meet the girl with no past, live happily ever after. I was lucky enough to know some of the others. Most of them still lived in town. I walked over to 7-Eleven to see if any were drunk yet.

They were.

Kurt and Lunchbox sat in the back of a pickup truck, passing a bottle back and forth.

"I cleaned a pool with Frankie Gunnz yesterday," Kurt said to me.

"How was that?"

"I got fired."

"First day?"

"Yeah. First day. Three hours."

"I thought I was in bad shape."

"You should ask him *why* he got fired," Lunchbox said.

"All right, Kurt," I leaned against the bed and got ready for a good one. "What did you do?"

"I lit the Boss' wife's cigarette."

"Before you lit yours?"

"Well ... yeah. Since when is that a crime?"

"What kind of cigarettes was she smoking?"

"I don't know. Whatever people smoke."

"Well, everyone knows the Boss' wife has a reputation for being 'friendly' with the help. If she's a smoker why didn't she have her own lighter?"

He didn't say anything.

"She didn't have her own cigarettes either," I said. "Did she?"

"No."

"You gave her a cigarette *and* you lit hers first?"

"People light each other's cigarettes all the time."

I stuck a cigarette in my mouth and motioned for a lighter. Kurt handed me one.

"That's true," I said. "But you're fresh meat. You knew exactly what she was after."

"So what? I should've been rude and not given her a cigarette?"

"No, you should always be polite. But keep some distance. Light yours first."

"The Boss is just jealous."

"That may be. But he can fire you. He can't fire her."

"You're saying he wasn't out of line?"

"I'm saying I just put a cigarette in my mouth, and you didn't light it for me."

He smiled like being cute was going to buy him some sympathy. "Well, that's what the Boss gets for hemmin' and hawin' all day with everyone but his wife. She got bored and ..."

"And there was good ole' Kurt to keep her company."

"Too bad I wasn't there," Lunchbox said. "Middle-aged women love me. I think I remind them of their high school boyfriends ... or sons."

"Even if I did cross a line, that's still no excuse to fire me. People need jobs."

I looked at my friend with no sympathy left to give. "Kurt, I've lit a lot of cigarettes for a lot of women. And my intentions were never good."

2

That night I went on a dating site. I made a profile and clicked "yes" and "no" to things that weren't true, but I wished they were. My evenings began to fill up with strangers who went by "CherishKisses" and "Love-to-Laugh-86." It was my moment. Things were finally starting to go my way.

I was back home at the Jersey Shore and I figured, why not? Broke and unemployed meant a lot of free time. Online dating seemed like the next logical step for a future in my parents' basement. And who knows, I thought, maybe one of these girls can teach me French.

It started well, I guess, but I could only drink so many pints, smoke so many cigarettes. And while the kegs changed, the girls didn't do much but complain about the current job market. I was growing restless again.

My dates hadn't heard of socialism. One thought Kurosawa was a motorcycle. None of them spoke French.

3

I moved the rest of my college boxes into my parents' basement. The dog didn't even lift her head as I walked by. She had the droopy eyes and droopy mouth of a boxer.

I crouched down and clapped my hands. "Satine, who's the best dog?"

Her cropped tail did a half-wag, a wag of annoyance.

I've even managed to disappoint the dog, I thought.

I pissed seven or eight times out of boredom and too much coffee. There were a few weeks' worth of *TIME* magazines on the toilet tank. I picked one up and started reading about a Tunisian fruit vendor who had lit himself on fire. Just as I was getting inspired, my mother knocked on the door.

"What are you doing in there?"

I ignored her.

She kept knocking. Her fist banged in a way that built in volume with each hit.

"I just watched a documentary on kids drinking Robitussin," she said. "Are you drinking Robitussin?"

That's not a bad idea, I thought.

I found a bottle in the back of the medicine closet. An old bottle. Dried goo had crystallized around the rim. I took two big gulps and looked out the window, waiting for *something* to happen. The world didn't look very interesting.

I felt like it was time to ask my father for advice.

"Get a job," he said.

"What job?"

"A job with a pension."

I left home and went back to 7-Eleven. My friends were sitting in the back of the pickup again. Same spot. Same clothes. Actually, I wasn't sure if they'd ever even left.

"Has 7-Eleven made you sign a lease yet?" I asked.

"I can't go home," Lunchbox said. "My dad caught me stealing his pills. He says I can't come back until I pass a piss test."

"What've you been doing?" Kurt asked me.

"I don't know. Trying to fall in love. Staring at a lot of walls. Thinking about writing a novel."

He laughed. "You can't be a writer."

"Why not?"

He poured a small bottle of whiskey into a flask and handed it to Lunchbox. "You don't wear enough black."

I got into the bed and sat between them. Then I took the flask from Lunchbox and swallowed a few times. "Maybe you're right."

"You're pretty good looking, though," Kurt continued. "It's always nice to have *that* ace in the hole."

"Why do you want to be a writer anyway?" Luchbox asked. "Reading sucks."

"The only thing I ever read was *The Road Not Taken* by Robert Frost," Kurt said.

I smiled at the memory of reading the poem back in middle school. "That poem made me think there are rewards for people who don't sell out."

"I got an F on the book report. That's when I realized school was stupid and they don't teach you anything important."

"And look how you turned out," Lunchbox said to him. "The only kid our age without any student debt."

"See that?" Kurt pointed a finger gun at me. "No book is going to tell you this stuff."

A Mini Cooper pulled into the handicap spot. Kurt and Lunchbox stopped talking and watched the car.

"What's the matter?" I asked.

"That's Queen Jac," Lunchbox said.

"I haven't seen her since high school."

"You don't forget that kind of beauty. Most people don't see it twice in a lifetime."

I thought about the first time my eyes had set on the Queen, back when my homeroom teacher introduced her to our class halfway through sixth grade. The feeling I'd gotten watching the fluorescent lights reflect off her braces was locked in the same drawer with the first time I tasted an oyster. It was like my whole life had been a desert that suddenly turned green.

"I hear her boyfriend has an ego so big it wouldn't fit into a flyover state," I said.

"Ex-boyfriend," they said together.

"I played her a Loretta Lynn song once on guitar," I frowned. "She hugged me."

"She had that three-way junior year behind the dugout," Kurt said. "Coach Ski got fired for taking pictures."

"I forgot about that."

"She took my virginity Senior Week," Lunchbox smiled. "What a week."

"I forgot about that, too."

"It wasn't very good. And now she pretends she doesn't even know me."

"Lunchbox," I said, "I'm learning sometimes you just can't win."

She stepped out of her car with skinny legs that disappeared into white cut-off jean shorts. I felt the whole world turn yellow, or whatever the color of music is. It was a high only the Queen could bring out of me. Sometimes life hands you your destiny in sixth grade. The smoke spells out her name. She's the saint chosen to erase all your sorrows. For better or worse, your soul will forever glow with a patina only one girl could've imbued.

Of course, the other party involved has to under-stand the rare handouts of the Universe too.

"She's single now?" I asked.

She was.

Well, why not, I thought, when you've got nothing, you've got nothing to lose.

I hopped off the truck. No guts and all heart. Ready to promise a lifetime of trips to the zoo. And endless picnics, so we could feed all the animals in the park.

The Queen froze when she saw me.

"I'd forgotten you existed until right now," she said.

"Good. A lot's changed since high school."

A playing card was lying face down next to her feet. I picked it up. The two of Hearts.

I said some of the right things. I asked some of the right questions. That night I was canceling with "Starlight84" and taking Queen Jac out for drinks.

4

We hit an Irish bar called The Shooter Shack with two-for-one Grey Goose specials. She wanted to go bowling, but I didn't have that kind of money.

"I'll buy the first round," she said. "I don't want you thinking this is a date."

We sipped our drinks in silence. I was giving off the distinct stench of a complete loser. And it was complem-ented, perfectly, with the DJ turning on my least favorite song: "Shot Through The Heart."

But the Queen's eyes went wide with the opening line, and she threw her hands in the air and said, "I love this song. Dance with me."

There's a look that beautiful women give when they

hit that top-shelf vodka-drunk. Like some country song in their head is playing at 90 BPM and only they can hear it. Head nodding back and forth. Eyes closed. Hair tucked over one ear. As bored with men as they are with music. But someone still gets to take them home. And this time, I figured, why not me?

The distortion of time.

In high school I could barely keep eye contact with her. But after seven vodka-clubs I was standing on a bar stool, holding her hand, and reciting poems from the French class I'd failed my first semester.

And then I managed my greatest feat: I got us back to my parents' house without crashing the car.

We landed on the futon in the basement, I think. At least, that's where my mom found us naked the next morning. The Queen lifted her head and a crust of drool cracked between her mouth and my chest. She looked at my mother through a cloud of too much vodka and said, "If I weren't so hung over I'd be really embarrassed."

5

I was homeless before dawn. And since my parents paid my car insurance, well, that was gone too.

My mom drove the Queen home and my father said I'd better be gone before she got back.

"What about the orchid I bought her?" I asked him. "Doesn't that get me a pass?"

"You drained that well days ago."

He gave me a $20 bill and I packed a bag with a Moleskine and a pair of clean socks. Then I headed out into the world. Alone. A total letdown to those who shared my name.

The hangover started to bend my brain as I paced

around town, cycling through the contact list on my phone, begging anyone who would answer to give me a couch for the night.

Frankie Gunnz said, "Rock n' roll, bro," but he couldn't pick me up for a few hours because a homeless guy had broken into the town's pool club and drowned. And he had to drain all the water before he could leave.

I told him I'd be at 7-Eleven and went to see if Kurt and Lunchbox were getting an early start. They weren't, but I found a bagged copy of *The New York Times* in the parking lot. I sat down on the curb and read there while Frankie earned a living.

6

Dusk fell and my eyes finally began to focus.

"I'm sorry that took so long," Frankie said. "I spent five hours pulling that homeless dude's hair out of the filter. I probably got AIDS."

"Don't apologize to me," I said. It wasn't often that I found time to read the paper. I'd made it all the way through the *Dining* section and ripped out a recipe for rabbit stifado. The hangover made cooking a meal like that for the Queen seem totally reasonable.

***

I hadn't seen Frankie in almost a year before running into him at Home Depot. Not since last summer at The Shooter Shack, the same bar Queen Jac and I had just shared our first kiss. It was right in the Mexican part of town, an old bucket of blood. I tried to avoid the area, but a shot wheel you could set your watch to started spinning at 11 p.m.

If your funds were low it was a risk worth taking.

Frankie had been romancing a real creature that night. His eyes flared when he saw me and he shoved his date behind the bar. A few minutes later the bartender slid a pint my way. It was a good faith pint from Frankie, I figured, to forget what I'd seen.

As I was paying my tab I saw a crowd gathering at the other end of the bar. A hairy mutant stood in front of Frankie. He was a local scumbag we all used to call Columbine (he got kicked out of our middle school for flushing a pipe bomb down a toilet). But in a noble embrace of his reputation he grew out his curly black hair until it formed one mass with his curly black beard. And now that he looked like a blow-dried Newfoundland, everyone called him The Beard.

I was pretty sure I could smell him from across the bar. He always had a particular funk of pedophilia and OxyContin's surrounding him like an invisible mold.

"That's my ex-girlfriend," The Beard pointed at Frankie's date.

"Oh yea?" Frankie said. "Well, don't worry. I promise I'll take good care of her."

The Beard threw his chest into Frankie. He didn't follow it with a fist or anything. They just looked at each other. Everyone in the bar was looking at them.

"You get one more of those," Frankie said. "Then it's going to be a midnight movie."

I almost felt bad for The Beard. Being labeled the town lunatic had probably encouraged in him a sense of false confidence his whole adult life. His battle plan started and ended with intimidation. But he hesitated on the draw, and Frankie saw it.

He chest bumped Frankie again. Harder this time.

Frankie smiled, having already given fair warning.

He pulled his shirt off and handed it to his date. The ink of the Italian flag between his shoulders seemed to sparkle especially bright under those bar lights.

"I warned you, Columbine," he said. "Now you're going to get raped in front of the whole town."

I grabbed my pint glass like a brick and headed toward the action. If Frankie ended up in trouble I wanted to get a decent shot in to help him out.

But Frankie Gunnz could go from zero to one hundred like something provoked and cold-blooded. The Beard had set the menace loose. Frankie's shaved skull flew through the air like a missile. The headbutt shattered The Beard's nose, and blood dripped from each hole in thick globs.

They grappled at the shoulders and rolled through the bar like two hungry dogs. Everyone in their way dodged the mess; no one even flirted with the risk of stopping them. Then the door opened and a mass of sweat, blood, and everything else that could fly from the noses and mouths of combat landed on the sidewalk.

It was the kind of Jersey Shore fight that crowned legends.

The bar crowd followed them outside and formed a circle. The Beard's face began to look like someone who'd stood too close to a parrot cage and gotten their nose chopped off. Weaker stomachs turned away. Real psychotics cheered. Even the Mexicans on the corner could be heard whispering: "Ay dios mio."

Sirens started blaring from blocks away. I saw the bartender push his face against the window and do a back-and-forth scan of the street. No cops yet. He shut off the lights and dropped the shades like no one was home.

An eruption came from The Beard that froze any

warmth left in the salty bay air. It was the sound of final acceptance - the deep hollow wail of an animal that had stared into its future and accepted doom.

"Frankie," I yelled. "I'm getting my car started. The Law's coming."

I knew he couldn't hear me. He had hit that red level, and I don't think he would've been able to recite the course of events even after a night's sleep and a cup of coffee. His arms looked like two oil drills. Pumping up and down. Up and down.

I was parked right across the street. I hopped in my car and got the wheel ready to swing a U-turn. Then I rolled the window down. "Frankie, we've got to scram, dude."

He didn't look up. The cop lights started coloring the street. Frankie was going down and I understood why. Had it been a regular fight, he would've gone until he'd won and then walked away. But this hairy goon had insulted Frankie, disrespected him with that chest bump on *his* own turf. No second chance for The Beard, and no quarter given.

I turned my car off and got out.

A police cruiser parked on the sidewalk in front of the bar. A cop stepped out and watched the fight for a minute.

"ALL RIGHT!" he ordered.

Frankie kept punching. I could see the cop's brain swelling. He was a hardened Irishman used to getting his way the first time around.

The cop pulled out his baton and walked toward Frankie's legs. He lifted it above his head and brought it down on the back of Frankie's knee. Frankie didn't react. He did the same thing to the back of Frankie's other knee.

Nothing.

The cop was so horny for violence it looked like he might bury two deep in the back of Frankie's head.

He put the bat away and took out a can of mace.

I clapped my hands to try and break Frankie's concentration. "Frankie, he's got the mace. Run!"

The cop bent down to eye level with Frankie and pulled the trigger. A white liquid squirted out with a loud *hiss* and hit him dead on.

"MY EYES," Frankie cried. "You killed my eyes. Cease fire!"

Two more cop cars pulled up on the sidewalk. All four doors of both cars opened and a potato-faced boy in blue sprung out from each one.

Frankie put his palm on The Beard's face and used it as a lift off. Then he took off for the marsh.

The cops struggled behind him for about ten feet. They dropped off one by one and leaned against each other and coughed until they caught their breath.

I got back in my car and headed home.

No reason to be accused of accessory, I thought.

7

Bayonne was the only place left that a working twenty-four-year-old could afford to live. Frankie rented out a mother-daughter with a big concrete stoop. The house was owned by an old Italian couple that lived on the second floor. "I have everything I need in there," Frankie said to me. "A futon and a dresser full of pool clothes."

Frankie had been at work since 5 a.m., but even after the long day he picked me up at 7-Eleven without any grief. A plastic bag was taped around the passenger window frame of his car. Someone had kicked in the window and stolen his E-ZPass a few days ago. The plastic bag had been holding off the elements, but as the car climbed the Newark Bay Bridge the wind changed direction, and the bag started jabbing my face like a boxing glove.

The blue-eyed Queen and her Grey Goose. What a thing to be punished for, I thought.

I looked over at Frankie and realized I'd never done anything for him, but when these situations arose, he was always the man to call. Frankie Gunnz. And he never asked for anything in return.

He was the right kind of guy for his place and time. An ultimate badass in a land of weak losers. If you looked through the albums at the bottom of his car you'd only find the classics: Dion and the Belmonts. Sinatra. And it was very rare to see anything playing on his parents' television other than *Goodfellas* or *Casino*. I made him watch *The Godfather* movies once. He liked I and II, but in the middle of III he turned off the TV and said, "Francis Ford should have said, 'You are not a good actress, Sophia,' and been done with the whole thing. It's becoming a cancer in my head, how something like this could happen."

Frankie knew someday it might occur; something so grotesque committed by his own hands that he would need three or four strong dudes to scrub the blood out. And when it comes to those crimes, only the most loyal of dogs can be trusted to take the guilt to the grave. It went unspoken, but I knew the day might come when I would have to take a major hit for all of Frankie's charity.

I wondered if he knew I'd already accepted this, or did our Guinea genes just act on instinct? Either way, his floor was always open when my parents kicked me out.

My father confiscated my "emergency" credit card this time too, and said, "If you're old enough to disrespect my house with a Keansburg tramp, you're old enough to live off your own dime."

8

I could see the Pulaski lights burning red through the smokestacks that rise along the banks of Newark Bay. Like ancient cannons pointing straight up toward the graveyard of a polluted night where nothing seems permanent enough to be dead. Not even choking stars. Just a black desolation blanket, soundless in the stone air. And as we crossed the Skyway, with Newark in our rearview and the lights and smells of a million sweaty workers crawling through rush hour, it all seemed completely in order. Like this had happened thousands of times before and would continue this way until the eternal sundown.

We hit a red light at the Rainbow Projects in Jersey City. A few corner boys were getting their pit bulls ready to massacre a crate of baby chickens.

Frankie had Sinatra's *Greatest Hits* playing on the stereo. He turned the volume up on "Coffee Song" and sang to the corner boys in a barbaric tone:

"You date a girl and find out later
She smells just like a percolator
Her perfume was made right on the grill
They could percolate the ocean in Brazil"

For some reason, Frankie's singing reminded me of The Beard's bleeding face. "You know, Frankie," I said, "I never found out what happened that night you ran from the cops."

His face bore the clear pride of insurrection. "Those fucking douche bags should've spent a few more hours on the treadmill if they wanted to catch Frankie Gunnz."

I already knew what happened that night, though. But not from any police blotter. Suburban lore spreads fast when it finally finds a hero.

After Frankie beat The Beard's face into canned tuna, he actually made it all the way to the marsh. He tread water for twelve hours. Blind from the mace. Crippled from the bat. Eventually he got bored and walked to the police station and turned himself in.

The cop who had maced Frankie laughed like he'd won something. Frankie laughed back in an orange jumpsuit. With shackles on his wrists and shackles on his ankles. He looked right at the cop and said, "This is what bravery looks like. Now you'll know it next time you see it."

They tried to block Frankie from a bail hearing, but he was released an hour later. On his way passed the mace cop, Frankie laughed again. "I forgot to mention," he winked. "My uncle's the mayor."

Frankie's mother cooked lasagna for dinner that night. His father said Grace and during dessert Frankie relayed the story from the night before.

"Those bastard cops," his grandmother said. "Every one of them. Filthy mutts."

"It's all right, Grandma," Frankie said. "They have jobs to do like the rest of us."

9

Frankie wanted to take me to a diner in Hoboken. He said they would still let us smoke inside, and only there could we reassess the crossroad at which I'd arrived.

I was starting to understand a universal irony - the world does not exist in the snow globe of a Robert Frost poem. The road less traveled ends in welfare checks and parking tickets. And the path that *is* paved has you owing your parents for car payments and student loans the rest of your life. It's how well you can bluff this awful hand that makes all the difference.

10

I ripped the plastic bag out of the window while we drove across Jersey City. Frankie skipped ahead through the Sinatra CD until he found "My Way." When the crescendo came, he raised both of his arms like a champion. The car seemed to follow the melody as we bounced along the missing cobblestones in the streets. The early spring air blew in through the open windows, working to thaw the cracks and fading eyes of our youth, the always hollowing places where cold burrows deep.

I stuck my head out the window and let the cool wind pull back on my hair. I looked across the Hudson at the bright lights of New York City, like a big blinking baby with eyes fighting gravity before the final exhale. The trains and taxis humming over the water rumbled the city streets like the mouth of a dreaming dog. Even the polluted cloud line smiled a soft green.

11

There were big NO SMOKING signs in every window of the diner.

"I guess that's it," Frankie threw his hands up in the air. "Everything our forefathers fought for is gone."

I followed him through the front door. A bowl of unwrapped mints sat on the hostess stand. Frankie stuck his hand in the bowl and grabbed some.

"Don't eat those," I said.

"Why not? They're delicious."

"What if the person before you just jerked off?"

"Who would do something that evil?"

"There're all kinds of people out there. Most of them are terrible."

We sat down. A waitress came over and dropped two menus on our table. Each had a Post-it Note with a stamped **X** over a hand-drawn cigarette.

"I can't believe it," Frankie said to me. "I was smoking in here last week."

"Everyone sells out eventually."

"Well, I'm ready to commit a chicken genocide. There'll be a poster of my face in every slaughterhouse tomorrow."

Frankie understood my situation and offered to pay without my asking. I ordered a Budweiser and a pork roll, egg, and cheese. Keep it simple, I thought, get your protein up.

But Frankie looked at the menu like he was going to *the chair* and ordered twice from every food group. Two pork roll, egg, and cheeses. Twenty chicken wings doused in Sweet Baby Ray's. A kebab. Disco fries. Extra coleslaw. Extra pickles.

The waitress asked Frankie if he was sure.

"Just keep them coming in twos," he said. "And for dessert, I'll have a strawberry milkshake."

"My favorite," the waitress smiled.

"It's my act of contrition to Saint Laurence. I missed Mom's homemade raviolis tonight."

Frankie's discipline inspired me. I told the busboy to

return with more beer.

"I think I should apologize to my parents," I said to Frankie. "Then I can just go home. I'd rather have them feeding me while they hate me."

"Not this time, bro. Stay with me. We'll live like the old days."

"I only have $20. How am I going to eat?"

"You could get a job."

"I don't have any more clothes. Or all the stupid documents you need to prove you're an American."

"Don't worry about any of that. Come work with me. Pool boys are always in demand."

This seemed like another problem on a big list of problems.

"I can't be a pool boy," I said. "I hate pools."

"I was going to make my little brother come work since Kurt got fired. But he can wait until next season."

"I'm not your man, Frankie. I'm barely *a* man."

"Bro, this is the best gig. You get to wear a bathing suit to work. Your tan will be sick. All the moms hang out in bikinis. All their daughters hang out in bikinis. And don't forget, cash pay."

"Pool boys?"

"Pool boys."

CHAPTER FOUR

1

There was frost on the ground when we got to the pool truck yard.

We'd left Bayonne around 5:00 a.m. for a 5:30 arrival. A straight shot down the Turnpike (exit 11) and then exit ramp onto the Garden State Parkway (exit 129). Our destination was a parking lot in Cliffwood Beach (exit 120).

Last night, after we gavoned everything at the diner, we stopped at the Rainbow Projects for some weed. The corner boys were cleaning up pieces of chicken gizzards. Their dogs looked at us with cloudy eyes; feathers and blood clotted their jowls like a malevolent growing moss. Frankie said he'd pay for the weed if I promised to keep him awake on the ride to work this morning.

At 11:00 p.m. that seemed totally doable, so I'd promised.

I lasted about two minutes on the morning commute before I was snoring away. I didn't even make the Turnpike.

The door on my side of the car opened from the

outside. Frankie leaned over me and coughed in my face while he unbuckled my seatbelt. Then he pulled me out the open door and let me fall headfirst onto the concrete. A frozen glaze of morning dew stung my cheek like a hot iron, but I knew it would only get worse from there so I didn't move.

"It's freezing," I said to him.

"I love the morning chill. Wait until noon. You'll be begging to jump in a pool."

Frankie cursed about global warming as he walked away and left me half-asleep on the concrete. I closed my eyes and saw my grandfather's face, ¼ paralyzed from a bullet in Bastogne, and a voice over somewhere, asking, "*For What?*"

Frankie started mixing death threats in with his curses and I didn't want to test him this early in the morning. I sat up and leaned against his bumper. We were in a parking lot full of scrap metal and old American cars. In the back section, I could see a huge chain-linked fence surrounding a fleet of pool trucks.

Glass began cracking all around us.

"What's that sound?" I asked.

"The Boss leases the back lot off of a used car company," Frankie said. "But they're always getting robbed, so they keep the cars stocked with Rottweilers."

The dogs were smashing their heads against the windows, trying to kill us. They were either starved or brainless. No hesitation as scabs opened and blood and humid dog breath fogged up the windows.

I rubbed my pupils until I could see, then I made peace with the sky. The time had come - I had walked right into perdition. The sun didn't even want any part of this terrible dawn. It hid behind a canopy of gray. I lit a cigarette, but when I tried to inhale my lungs closed and

I coughed out huge plumes of carbon monoxide.

5:35 a.m. and I was already looking for an escape.

Frankie threw me a bathing suit and a pair of flip flops from the back of his car. "Put those on," he said. "They're yours for the rest of the season."

"Why do we have to be the first ones here?" I asked. "Couldn't we have slept another twenty minutes?"

"I like people knowing I got here first. It keeps everyone else on their toes."

"Are you getting paid more than them?"

"No."

"Then I'll take a bus tomorrow. I don't need to suffer because you're the only person in the world who wants to work hard."

A row of barbed wire ran on top of the fence that stood between us and the pool trucks. Frankie jumped up, grappled some chain, and climbed the fence like a spider. Then he pulled off his sweatshirt and spread it over the barbed wire.

I refused to follow him on grounds of exploitation.

"We're crossing the Great Wall of China to get into work?" I said. "People have given their lives to take this kind of power away from bosses."

I waited while he climbed around and opened the gate.

Frankie had been telling me bits and pieces about the Boss for years. The legend went something like this: the Boss was a real flag-saluting casualty of the free market. With some ambition (and a decent settlement from a drunk driving pile-up), he built a pool company from his parents' living room. He could buy his wife a new car now, but it came at the price of having to watch his kids grow up on the internet for half the year. If Frankie showed up early and got the basic operations in order, the Boss could sleep-in and eat breakfast with his kids. There was no reward for Frankie in any of this, but sometimes it's about doing *the right thing.*

Or so he said.

A key was left for Frankie under a dumpster. It opened a green shipping container that doubled as the office and supply room.

We walked in and I saw a mini keg of Coors Light sitting on a desk. A poster of a guy asleep with his head in a toilet was stuck to the wall. A Polaroid picture was tacked to the poster. It was of a different man, asleep with his head in a toilet. Someone had written **THE BOSS IN COLLEGE** on the Polaroid in black Sharpie.

I held the keg hose and took a decent gulp. Frankie found a bin in the back of the trailer and pulled out a gray Guinea-tee. "American Pools" was typed across the chest.

"That is the stupidest name I've ever heard," I said.

"People love America."

"But it doesn't even make sense. Why are we getting patriotic about pools?"

"Who knows? Who cares? Put it on."

I put it on. A Guinea-tee, bathing suit, and flip flops somehow came together as a uniform.

I'm not sure why, but it made me angry.

I took another solid chug from the keg hose. It was all starting to become clear. I had hit the end. The bosses. The cold dawns. The next sixty years would start just like this. And one lucky day, I would die.

I lit a cigarette and pulled out my phone to text someone. But who? The Queen? We did sleep together. I was sure of that. But I couldn't remember if I'd made her finish, and we'd been robbed of the brunch where I could promise next time would be better.

Quit while you're ahead, I thought. Leave her alone.

Frankie backed a white Toyota pickup to the door of the trailer. He got out and pet the side like it was a show pony. "This is mine," he said. "I set the record every Saturday in this baby."

"Is today Saturday?"

"Hell yeah, bro. We're going to clean more pools than anyone else in this lot."

"No ..."

"If we don't stop for lunch we should be home by nine."

"Nine?" I stuttered. "P.M.?"

"Nice easy day," he gave me a thumbs up. "But if any of those side-wiping faggots left a single fast food wrapper in my truck again, I'm quitting."

Frankie prided himself on a work ethic unseen in civilizations not practicing manumission. A side effect of a very clear reptilian complex. But he was also a man who abided by the strictest code of honor. One that drew lines in the sand which could never be pushed back. All the other employees denied guilt, but *someone* had taken Frankie's pickup out last week and left it filled with Wendy's wrappers and squeezed condiments.

"Really?" I asked. "You'll quit?"

"I swear to God I'll quit."

"If you do, we should go right to a motel and sleep for a couple hours."

"Get the truck packed up," he said. "I'm buying some lottery tickets. I need to read my horoscope today. I'm feeling lucky."

He gave me a fist pound. Then he went across the street to a deli.

A sheet of paper hung from the wall reminding employees what to load into the truck: One bucket with forty pounds of chlorine. One bucket full of Diatom-aceous Earth (D.E. is a white powder poured into the pool filter to suck up dirt and debris). One garbage can with a thirty-foot hose. One garbage can with a fifteen-foot hose. One pool pump (a one horsepower Hayward motor). One reserve pump for additional filtration (looks like R2-D2). One filter. One power washer. One crate full of small shock bags. Three backwash hoses. Vacuum pole. Skimmer pole. Vacuum heads. Brush heads. A clip-board with receipts and bills. And road maps of the greater Monmouth County, NJ area.

2

Frankie came back with a newspaper and a bag full of water bottles. He climbed into the passenger side and dropped the bag on the floor. Then he pulled a handful of lottery tickets from his pocket and started scratching.

Getting all the cargo to fit into the truck bed was about as complicated as a 1,000-piece jigsaw puzzle. I ended up making it work, but then I had to pull bungee cords across to keep everything holstered in. On the last one, just as I was about to click the clasp through the hole, something snapped and the hook shot at me. It hit my ear like a bullwhip and I went down cursing right into the cold pavement. It made the dogs crazy and their barks served as some awful suburban alarm clock, like rabid roosters settling a score with the dawn.

Frankie came over to me and pulled a roll of duct tape from his pocket. He tore off a three-inch piece, pushed it against my bleeding ear, and said, "Leave that on for a few days and it should heal itself."

"Those dogs are driving me nuts."

"Hey, don't get mad at them. *You* got them all worked up. They caught *your* blood scent."

"We should open up packets of chlorine and shove them up the tailpipes," I said. "The dogs will just drift off to sleep."

"The Boss is hemorrhaging money all over the place. He already made a rule about wasting chemicals."

The goddamn economy. It was what led to this whole mess in the first place. Had my mother been employed, the Queen and I could've just slept off our hangovers. I thought about what she might've looked like: makeup a complete mess, stockings all ripped and torn. And me, waking up with a mouthful of her hair, rubbing my finger around her hip bones to circle each goose bump that rose with the silent compliment of helpless orgasm.

The list of failures had no ceiling.

3

The Boss drove into the parking lot on a purple Harley. He took off his Oakley sunglasses and smiled at us. A white tan line stretched from his eyes to ears. Like an albino raccoon.

"Sorry I'm late, boys," he said. "The wife's three months pregnant. She's already fat as hell, and I can't keep her off me."

I thought about my unemployed friend getting ready for another day drinking at the 7-Eleven. Poor Kurt. With the Boss' wife all charged up like that a mountain of Catholic guilt couldn't have saved him.

"If any politician actually cared about us they would pass the only law we really need," Frankie said. "Every workday starts with blowjob hour."

"Count me out," the Boss said. "My wife hasn't

been this horny since prom night. I can't take it."

"I didn't even get laid on prom night," I said.

"You're lucky," he frowned. "I've been stuck with her ever since."

We followed the Boss into the shipping container. He sat at his desk and took out a pack of E-Z Widers and a copy of the *Daily News*. Frankie broke up some weed and rolled a joint while the Boss yelled "SON-OF-A-BITCH" at each page of the newspaper.

Frankie passed the joint to the Boss and lit it for him. The Boss took a deep inhale and motioned for the lighter. Then he took another pull. Then another.

"Are you going to pass that?" I asked him.

He looked at Frankie. "Who's this guy?"

"My friend, Londi," Frankie said. "He needs a job."

"What do you do?" the Boss asked me.

"I write. Sometimes."

"Do you know anything about pools?"

I looked at Frankie, waiting for a hint.

"No," I said.

"Tools?"

"I took a guitar apart once."

"I guess that's good enough. I have to hire every one of my wife's degenerate brothers, anyway. It's $10 an hour. And if you see my wife, stay away."

"Is there any sort of pension plan involved?" I asked. "Or 401k, maybe?"

The Boss laughed. Frankie laughed. The Boss raised his hand, hovered it around Frankie's face, then slapped it against Frankie's jaw and held it there. "Pension plan," he said. "Frankie, this kid's in the wrong line of work. Get him on a stage. Make some real money."

The Boss kept laughing and the joint went out. He opened another drawer in his desk and pulled out a three-pound bag of Mike and Ikes.

"I stole this from Ralph," he said about the candy. "Talk about a booze bag. I bet I could get him to sign his house over for a Miller Light and a cheese sandwich. Ralph. That guy has a jackass diploma."

He took a picture out of his wallet and handed it to us. It was of him, his wife, and some other people around a birthday cake. He repeated "Ralph" and pointed at one of the guys in the picture.

"Here," he pushed the Mike and Ikes over to Frankie.

"Nice," Frankie said. "Original flavors."

I reached in the bag and came out with a pink one.

The Boss just about fell backwards out of his chair. "Strawberry! Strawberry's not an original flavor. It was orange. Lime. Lemon. Cherry." He brought his hand up and down for each flavor like he was hacking a board.

"You can't trust anything anymore," Frankie said. "Not your candy. Not your girl ..."

"Just your dog," I interrupted.

"And then the dog dies," the Boss said. "My dog died. Now what do I have?"

"The day my dog goes, I go." I did the sign of the cross. "That's it."

Frankie gave his condolences.

"Jesus, you two sound like a couple of homos," the Boss said. "I killed the goddamn dog."

I looked back at the photograph of the family around the birthday cake. There it was. A curious little basset hound with a happy face. A white dot right on the end of its nose. Some kid straddled the dogs back like a horse. His smile squinted his eyes and the whole thing made me terribly sad.

The Boss looked at my jaw, agape in horror. "Don't

tell me you're another one of those SON-OF-A-BITCH liberals?"

My head moved from side to side.

"My wife showed up one day with a dog," he said. "She found the thing in a park and wouldn't turn it in. All of a sudden I had a dog. I didn't want kids and I got those, too." He paused there like we would understand, then he lit the joint again and took a drag.

"I started getting itchy so I figured the dog gave me scabies," he continued. "I kept opening the door when my wife wasn't home but obviously the dog wasn't going anywhere. So one night I drank a case of beer. I held it all in until I thought my balls would burst. Then I climbed onto the couch. I pissed forever. I covered the whole couch in piss."

He took his index finger and tapped it against his temple, trying to convince us there was a brain somewhere in there. "My wife sat on the couch for one second and that was the end of the dog."

"You pissed on your own couch?" Frankie said. "And framed the dog?"

He grabbed the bag of Mike and Ikes back from Frankie and emptied a handful into his mouth. "Here's the part that's really fucked up. You can't catch scabies from a dog."

"What was it?" I asked him.

He gave some kind of welled up laugh and pieces of half-chewed candy goo shot out of his mouth. "My wife switched fabric softeners. It was just allergies. The poor dog died for nothing."

4

The radio in the truck didn't work and I passed out

before Frankie was done fighting with the Boss over the route.

He hit my elbow with a metal clipboard and I woke up.

"Did you quit?" I asked.

"No."

"You should've thrown a dung grenade at that dog killer, Frankie." I reached under my seat and pulled out an old Wendy's wrapper. "And there's a Wendy's wrapper under my seat. Show some backbone."

"I thought about it, but I'm going to get him back instead."

"How?"

"He gave us nine stops. But we're going to finish them fast and call him for more."

"That's the worst idea I've ever heard."

"No, bro. I'm going to show him I can't be beaten. Nobody's better than Frankie Gunnz."

We had seven pools to deal with and two money collections from people who had been dodging their bills. The route had us zigzagging the far corners of the county like a cursed treasure map. The Boss knew Frankie was the only one who could handle an assignment as involved as this. Frankie took it as a measure of good faith, but I knew better. We were getting the short end for a man's dedication to a job well done. If I had been an American Pools employee for more than an hour I would've spoken up.

But it was not the time to start a revolution. We were at the hour of annihilation. Locked in. Yesterday would have been the time to turn back. If I were to get in Frankie's head now the battle would still have to be waged. And if I had any chance of seeing the Queen again I needed to keep him moving like a three-legged ass-kicker. He was the kind of guy who could outrun a horse down the backstretch, so long as someone doubted that he could.

5

One opening.
> Four weeklies.
> One pool liner with hole.
> One mystery pool.
> Two collections.
> Nothing out of the ordinary for this time of year.

"We have to watch out for the collections," Frankie said. "Everyone just signs the receipts and swears they'll pay. But collection time means their checks bounced. The Boss said without the money there's no reason for us to come to work tomorrow."

The dogs attacked again on the way out.

CHAPTER FIVE

1

I asked the Arab guy filling up our gas tank, "How's it going, man?"

He looked at me like nobody had ever spoken to him before and said, "Same shit, different day."

He was wearing a name tag that said Carl. I felt like Carl and I were fighting the same war - servicing people we didn't like in a world we'd never get to enjoy.

"Same shit, Carl? Nothing different has happened?"

"I was asleep until you pulled in."

Frankie was out of the truck, smoking a cigarette in front of the gas station's bodega. Gas prices had risen and the Boss couldn't remember if there was enough money on the company debit card for a full tank. Frankie was doing jumping jacks and screaming into his cell phone: "I swear I'll quit. I'm not going to run out of gas on one of those hick-drool roads. It's a white trash classic out there."

I tapped Carl on his shoulder. He was watching Frankie punch the air.

"You better hold on," I said to him. "It sounds like

our company is going bankrupt."

The gas pump hit exactly $15. Enough for about twenty minutes in the environmental holocaust we were driving.

Carl pulled the hose out. Gasoline shot across the side of the truck and spilled all over the tire and ground.

"What the hell was that, man?" I said. "I was about to light a cigarette."

The price on the machine went up $.15 more.

"Hey," I pointed at the pump. "I saw that. We're not paying that."

"Yes. Yes. That is price."

This is what we get for all the Republicans saying, "Welcome to America, now speak ENGLISH." Immigrants, smarter than us, fluent in two languages.

"That is price?" I said. "You shit slump. You spoke perfect English two seconds ago."

"Yes. Thank you, sir. That is price."

"I know you understand what I'm saying."

A police car pulled up to another pump. I waved my arms at him. He pretended not to notice so I pounded the horn until he got out and gave me a little nod.

Carl was confident and silent.

"What's the problem?" the cop asked.

He was fresh out of the academy. A nice clean shave and a short blonde Nazi cut. The perfect foot soldier.

"This man is running the price up," I said.

He looked at Carl. "What's he talking about?"

Carl gave him a confused shrug.

"Pay him," the cop said to me.

"Pay him?" I was shocked. "He's swindling $.15 out of me and you're letting it happen?"

The cop didn't pretend to care. He looked at the price on the pump. "$15.15," he said.

"All right, Carl," I sighed, "looks like you win. Let me get the company card."

"Nope," the cop said. "Pay him now."

I took the $20 my dad had given me out of my wallet and handed it over. Carl pulled $4 from his pocket. He didn't have exact change.

Now he was stealing a whole dollar from me.

"That's all the money I have," I said. "I'm poorer than the camel herders you left back home."

I put my wallet away while Carl and the cop exchanged an obvious fraternal nod. Then I drove the truck over to Frankie. He opened the passenger door and said, "What the hell was all that?"

"I'm not sure. I think I was just the victim of an extortion operation."

I got out of the truck and traded places with Frankie. He climbed behind the wheel and readjusted the rearview mirror.

"Here comes the pig," he said. "Be cool."

The cop walked right past my window and went inside the bodega. We watched him stroll down each aisle. He took a bagel, a coffee, and a newspaper. He didn't even stop at the counter to pay. When he got back into his car, he lifted his coffee cup to Carl in a silent "thanks."

"It's like they *want* to be hated," Frankie said.

"You're not going to find an argument here."

He lit a cigarette and passed me one. "How much was the gas?"

"$16."

"Wow. That $20 went fast."

"Yeah. I only have $4 to my name. Do you think the Boss will give me an advance?"

"I doubt it. I've got enough cash to float us, though."

"How are we going to get more gas? We're barely above 'E'."

"The Boss' wife is putting money into all the accounts right now."

"I think the Boss has smoked himself stupid."

Frankie picked up the newspaper and scrolled to the horoscopes. He ran his finger down the list and said, "The Boss is an Aries."

"What does that mean?"

"He's got a head like a ram. It's a real curse. Hitler. Stalin. Lady Gaga. Aries are psychopaths with motivation."

"How do you know his birthday?"

"His wife made us go bowling last year for his fortieth."

"Why does everyone want to go bowling? I hate bowling."

"You wouldn't if someone else was paying for it."

"That's probably true."

"At least you have a few bucks left, though. $4 can probably get you a lifetime supply of Ramen Noodles."

"I have to call my parents and apologize."

"Bro, don't worry," he smacked his lips together as he pulled his cigarette out. "It's pool season. We're all good."

2

Frankie won $10 between two scratch-offs and offered to buy me breakfast at Dunkin' Donuts. I usually drank percolated coffee, the kind that could stimulate my pineal gland enough to turn me fourth dimensional. It would take maybe seven cups of Dunkin' Donuts coffee to get

me near that level. But since I was living off Frankie's
charity I didn't want to break the bank. So I took an
extra-large, black, and filled it up with eleven packets of
sugar.

Frankie interrupted while I was ordering a quesadilla
breakfast-goo sandwich. "Be careful, bro. You don't
want to start the day off with the shits."

"What do you eat for breakfast?"

A wicker basket was sitting on the counter. Frankie
reached in and pulled out six bananas on a stem. "You
eat six of these every morning and your ass will look like
mine."

The woman behind the counter leaned forward and
looked down at his ass.

"I'm fine with the goo sandwich," I said to her. "I
was blessed with the stomach of a Billy goat."

We ate in the truck and watched pigeons fight over
the remains of a McDonald's Happy Meal.

"I hate those birds," Frankie said. "They live entirely
on a garbage diet. And the more concrete you put in, the
more they keep coming."

I fell asleep while he was explaining pigeon behavior
and spilled my coffee all over myself and the newspaper.
It soaked right through my bathing suit and lit my crotch
on fire. I jumped out of the truck and ran to a patch of
grass with a sprinkler. Then I hit the ground and humped
the spout until I cooled off.

3

Frankie dug one of his old bathing suits out of the toolbox and tossed it to me. I changed behind the truck, but
the coffee was like tree sap on my skin. I'd need an ice
bucket by 3 p.m. for the jockage fire that was now inev-

itable.

"I guess I should warn you," Frankie said. "I think I had Chlamydia in that bathing suit once."

"I don't even share drinks with people because I'm afraid of getting a cold sore."

"If you do get it, it's nothing a few pills won't fix."

"I don't have health insurance."

I reached into the truck for my phone. In the twenty-four hours since I'd seen my parents all my money had been stolen, I'd eaten enough animal hormones to grow another arm, and now, I'd probably contracted an STI.

"I'm calling my mother," I said.

"Why don't you prove what kind of man you are first?"

"How?"

"You started something. Show them you can finish it."

I put the phone down.

"That's not such a bad idea, Frankie."

"Besides, Chlamydia is like the mosquito bite of STIs. Worst comes to worst your piss burns a little. Don't let it ruin your day."

4

"I think I love her," I said.

"Who?"

"Queen Jac."

"What's her sign?"

"Our birthdays are pretty close," I said. "I'm pretty sure she's a Libra. Like me."

"Libra is the only sign that can date itself. But nothing ever ends well, so who knows."

"I think she's been around before. Like this isn't her first life. She's got those old-soul blue eyes."

"Those are the ones you can't trust. They know how to play the game too well."

"I'm closer to the cusp. Whatever the next sign is."

"Scorpio. Fire sign. Another month with nothing but assholes."

Frankie's family moved to our town from Staten Island in sixth grade too, so he'd known Queen Jac as long as I had. He was even in the gym class that I'd failed for never bringing a change of clothes. I didn't tell anyone then, but I left them in my locker every day so I could sit on the bleachers with the Queen. She had a fake doctor's note playing up her asthma because she thought exercise was "so annoying" when you could just maintain an eating disorder.

I earned the F.

She passed.

I took it as a clear sign that we would grow old together. She won Prom Queen. And that was it. We didn't speak again until two days ago in the 7-Eleven parking lot.

"Bro, this sounds like the real thing," Frankie said. "I've got to take you guys out for dinner."

"We're not dating or anything. I don't even know if she's going to remember we hooked up."

"She woke up naked to your mom screaming at her. I'm sure she'll remember."

"You're right. What if she never talks to me again? Oh God. It feels like high school all over."

"You're freaking out. Open the glove box. There's a surprise in there."

I opened it. A mason jar full of yellow weed rolled out.

"Whoa," I said. "Wake and bake, bro."

I reached my hand into the air and Frankie high fived it.

"Wake and bake, bro." He pulled a book bag from behind his seat and handed it to me. "There's a lighter and a pipe somewhere in here."

He told me the weed was some new strain from California so I should only pack a little bit. The pipe was a little one-hitter painted like a cigarette. Perfect for clandestine rips. I jammed in as much weed as I could, took two hits, and passed it to Frankie.

Then I went back to sleep.

CHAPTER SIX

Weekly Service #1

1

A fog rose over the dawn of suburbia. There was nothing clean about this morning. Roadkill at every corner. Puddles of green scum bubbled with mosquito larvae in the sidewalk cracks. The smell of fresh mulch made us sneeze as it invaded the truck; donkey-shit and dirt dug like little razors into our nostrils.

I remembered the last time I had seen the world at this hour. After the late nights of college when I was lucky enough to have a few cigarettes left and a girl to walk home. Any excuse to avoid sleep. To let those few moments that fill the deep caverns of your soul live in the clean, raw morning. A dawn that can only be seen after you ask, "Why isn't there more night?" The ash and bone of a red Jersey dawn. Charred embers on the fringes of coming clouds. Filled with promise of more danger and more life when you wake up and start it all again. And then the new day comes, but like most moments in life, expectation betrays the victory.

Frankie let the truck roll down the street in neutral. He pointed at houses with pools as we drove by: "Above ground pool in that backyard. They've got an in-ground pool. Waterfall there. Solar cover on theirs. No cover on any of those."

It wasn't hot yet, but I could see thick mist burning off from behind the houses. The pools were already shooting off steam like they were on fire. A sure sign the day was going to roast us until our tongues flopped out of our mouths.

Frankie started nodding his head knowingly as we got closer to our first assigned pool. A little ranch sat back from the street behind some pine trees. It looked beat up; the tan vinyl siding had faded to a dull brown.

"I remember these knuckle-heads from last year," Frankie said. "There're pine trees surrounding the entire pool."

"So?"

"So, you're going to have to skim out every pine needle. And they're going to bitch because the needles will be blowing back into the pool while you're skimming."

Frankie pulled into the driveway and parked under a tree. He finished his cigarette and flicked it onto the yard. Then he stared angrily at the house, lost in an unblinking meditation.

"What's wrong with you?" I asked.

"I'm just trying to get pumped up. We're about to go to war."

"Well, we better make a move. If anyone's watching they're going to think we're casing the joint."

"Doesn't matter, bro. We're pool boys. Nobody can touch us." He opened his door and jumped down to the concrete. "I'll go check out the damage. Grab the Hayward and the reserve pump, three bags of shock, two poles, and maybe the filter … yeah, grab the filter. Better safe than sorry."

"Maybe I should just carry the whole truck into the backyard."

He hit his hand against his chest and mimicked my sarcasm back to me like he was an invalid.

"Hey, you actually sound smarter like that," I said.

"Jesus, I'm definitely going to hell for that one. All right, finish your cigarette, then meet me in the back."

I smacked the radio. It turned on this time with a bright flash but then dimmed like a lightbulb on its last watt. A morning talk show was in the middle of a prank call. They were trying to convince some mother that her daughter went to England and ended up pregnant in an orgy with The Rolling Stones. They brought the poor mother to tears before they stopped.

The moon must be about to split in half, I thought. The whole world has gone crazy.

I spun the channel dial until I found WSOU (89.5). Then I looked into the backyard of our first stop and saw Frankie. He was trying to smash the pool's heater box open with a rock.

The clock in the dashboard hadn't been changed for daylight saving time. A Bob Dylan song came on as it flashed 5:55. "They say the darkest hour comes right before the dawn," he sang. But I had been awake for that hour right before the light broke. It was a black desolation - an Old Testament pre-dawn - and as far as I could tell it hadn't led to any spiritual light. The world just seemed to be getting worse with each passing minute.

It was actually 6:55, real time. I looked at Frankie again. Then back at the clock. I thought of my parents.

Were my sins worth this penance? But then I pictured the Queen out on that dance floor, with her long neck and a waist I could meet my hands around right above her big ass. And her lips ... they curled up on one side when she was nervous and knew I was about to kiss her.

I grabbed the weed pipe and took enough hits to get myself properly mangled. Hell yeah this is worth it, I thought. A day of torture is a small price for a night of glory.

2

I was too high and lazy to make more than one trip from the truck to the backyard. So I carried the three bags of shock with my mouth, a pump per hand, and a pole under each armpit.

The pumps were the only hard part. They hung at ankle level. It took a few steps before I figured out how to balance everything without smashing my shins to pieces.

I left the filter behind, hoping Frankie wouldn't notice.

A dog was barking inside the house. It sounded like a little asshole with white fur and hard teeth. The kind of dog that was bred to kill a badger, and now with nothing to hunt, saves up all its carnage for the pool boy.

Terrific, I thought. This numbskull homeowner will probably let the dog out and say, "He's completely harmless," just in time for it to latch onto my big toe.

"Watch out, bro," Frankie shouted from over the fence. "There's dog shit everywhere."

His warning came as my foot went down on a mound of it. It felt like something only a mastiff could unload. My foot sank through without hitting the ground. A tidal wave of shit came over my flip flop and nestled between my toes.

I lost my momentum and one of the pumps hit my ankle. It ripped my skin off and blood ran down my leg. Flies immediately began landing on the shit curds that were stuck to my foot.

I dropped the bags of shock from my mouth. "Frankie," I yelled. "I need help, man. I'm in bad shape."

3

I sat on the diving board and looked at my shitty foot.

"What should I do?" I asked Frankie.

"Jump in the pool."

A blanket of pine needles covered most of the pool. But the mass didn't look thick enough to camouflage blood and poop.

"Really?"

He gave me a thumbs up. "Wake and bake, bro."

"Chlorine's strong enough to kill anything, right?"

"Dude, chlorine was a chemical weapon once. How do you think waterparks exist without everyone getting sick? Imagine what goes on in those."

I peeled the bloody duct tape off my ear and threw it in the grass. Removing it hurt even more than when the bungee cord had hit me.

"Your ear looks like eggplant parm," Frankie laughed. "That water's going to sting."

I walked to the edge of the diving board (blood running down my ankle and wet shit between my toes), bounced up, and did an impressive swan dive into the pool.

The arctic water hit me like a Pacquiao punch. Icicle snot poured out of my nose. Instinct tried to force me up, but I held my breath and drifted toward the bottom.

I opened my eyes when I got to the floor. Blood swam away in little pink ribbons. Both cuts felt like hot knives were being pressed against them.

As for the shit - it scraped off pretty easily against the bottom of that twenty-foot, kidney shaped, in-ground pool.

4

I swam to the edge of the pool and pulled pine needles from my hair while studying the sky. The gray clouds were starting to break open for an orange haze.

"When was the last time it rained?" I asked.

"It always looks like it's going to rain."

"Do we get to go home if there's a thunderstorm?"

"No way. Every pool is do or die."

"But if there's lightning we *will* die."

"Hasn't gotten me yet, bro. You live good, you live clean, good things happen."

It was barely seven and Frankie was already covered in sweat. He peeled off his Guinea-tee and dropped it in the grass. Then he tried fitting the rock he had used to knock open the heater box back into its groove.

"I don't know why I even bother," he said. "None of these idiots notice anything unless their pool is green when we leave."

I pulled myself out of the water, shaking off hypothermia. When the water flattened Frankie inspected the pool and said, "Good Lord." Footprint-sized skid marks of dog shit stuck to the floor like I'd stepped in brown paint.

"Make sure you vacuum all of that up," he pointed. "They might notice something like that."

I looked at the heap of pool supplies we had dump-ed in the backyard. I'll have to do this six more times, I thought.

"What should I do first?" I asked.

"Dump the filter baskets over the fence."

I scanned each corner of the yard. We were in a dev-elopment of taxpayers who couldn't afford the luxury of privacy. Other backyards bordered us on every side.

"If I dump the garbage over the fence it'll be in someone else's yard," I said.

"Just make sure no one's looking."

This kidney-shaped pool had two filter baskets, one on each side where the pool curved into itself. The bask-ets were supposed to catch everything that fell into the water and drowned.

I stuck my finger through the hole in the filter lid and jimmied it loose. The basket was floating about an inch under the water line, kind of on its side. It was full of dead spiders and a few furry creatures bloated like little balloons about to burst. I knew the mice wouldn't play dead, but spiders were a different story. There was no way I was sticking my hand in there and taking the chance.

I used the skimmer pole to jack the basket out of the water. It plopped down on the concrete with a wet slap. A million spider legs stuck out of the holes where the water drained.

I didn't see any noses pressed against the neighbor's windows so I picked the basket up and gave it two wha-cks against their fence. All the stinky glop fell out in one huge clump onto their yard.

I put my finger through the hole in the next filter lid and hit something. But it wasn't plastic; it moved with my touch. I jumped back and grabbed the skimmer pole in case I had to fight something off.

A big tarantula maybe.

"Frankie, there's something alive in here."

"Oh, hell yeah," he smiled. "I haven't found anything cool in a while."

He came over with a hammer and handed it to me. Then he stuck his finger into the hole and pulled the lid off.

Nothing lunged out. There were some more dead bugs and a big soggy brown vine bent around the filter basket.

"Damn, bro. You got me all excited."

I started to apologize, but then the brown vine began moving and we realized it was actually a coiled body unraveling itself.

"Hell's bells," I said. "It's so big I didn't even realize what I was looking at."

A Northeastern water snake was staring up at us like we'd woken it from a nice deep slumber. Its thick body made it look just like a cottonmouth. I knew it wasn't venomous, but the winter *had* run long this year. The snake probably hadn't eaten since October.

"I'll go inside and get a blow dryer," I said. "We can drop it in the water and blast this bastard back to hell."

Frankie looked at me like I'd made some grand insult. "I'm Frankie Gunnz," he said. "I don't need any help."

His hand dove into the filter like one of those arcade crane games - big claw wide open, zoning in, grappling down, getting it halfway up, and then dropping it.

The snake hit the concrete and hurled itself right up at me. I screamed and slapped it in the face. Then I dropped the hammer and jumped back into the pool.

When I surfaced, Frankie was cursing and running

around the backyard swinging the hammer down. "You slithering shit," he was saying. "I'll rip your teeth out with a screwdriver."

"That's right, Frankie," I cheered. "Kill it. Give the buzzards something to chew on."

He gave up and walked back to the pool clutching his forearm. Deep purple blood was seeping out from under his hand. His arm looked like a 3D map of the Amazon River. "I couldn't catch it," he growled. "What a way to start the morning."

"It looks like you fisted a porcupine. What happened?"

"You slapped the snake so hard it hit me like a two-pronged spear."

The snake's mouth had been open just enough to catch his arm on the way by, he said. Its teeth hooked him like a snagged fishing line, cutting clean through his skin and dragging almost from wrist to elbow. "Good to know," he scowled. "I'll never have you watching my back again."

He threw the hammer at me and jumped in the pool. But the blood pouring out of him was much thicker than what had come out of me. It didn't dissipate as quickly.

"Shit," he said. "We need to get rid of all this blood before the owner wakes up. It's starting to look like a Japanese bay after a dolphin slaughter."

5

The rest of the pool cleaning went off without a hitch.

Frankie excused himself and headed for the truck to duct tape his arm back together. He told me to dump six bags of shock into the pool when I was done. This was three more than necessary, he said, but he didn't want the snake returning anytime soon.

"At least if the snake comes back now the shock will melt it," he said. "Or it'll glow like an underwater flashlight."

I kept looking over my shoulder to see if the snake was lying in the grass, waiting to finish the job. But I finished vacuuming the pool without another sighting.

The vacuum connected to the Hayward pump by a thirty-foot hose. Water was pulled from the pool through the vacuum and blasted around a basket to weed-out any debris. A PVC pipe dumped the cleaned water from the pump back into the pool. But the pump had to be turned off and emptied every few minutes because of all the pine needles. They clogged the basket like a dam and blocked the suction.

By the time I dumped the last basket over the fence a dense mound of junk had formed. I broke a branch off the neighbor's bush and laid it on top of the pile. To make it look 'natural.' Then I unplugged the pump and brought everything back to the truck.

Frankie was sitting in the driver's seat looking like every ounce of his pride had been sucked out. "I hate snakes," he said to me. "I faced my fear and I still lost. I should've torn its eyes out of its skull."

"It's eight in the morning, man. I'm sure you'll have another chance."

Two children were selling lemonade in front of a neighboring house. Frankie looked like he was going to drive our truck through their stand. He didn't say anything. He just hit the weed pipe and kept staring at the kids.

If he wanted to knock their stand over what the hell did I care? I dropped the machines into the bed of the truck and went back to skim the pool.

6

Frankie was scribbling on his clipboard when I finished loading up the truck. He tore out a yellow piece of paper and showed it to me. "See this? This is the bill all the weeklies get. $120."

The handwriting on the yellow paper looked like hieroglyphics.

"Those don't even look like words," I said. "How do people read this?"

Frankie stuck the paper into the house's mailbox. "They don't. They can't. I can't. But as long as the pool is clean no one complains."

It was a good enough answer for me. I sat in the truck and smoked a cigarette. The pool had taken an hour, even with us working top speed to hide all the spilled blood.

"We've got to make up some time on the road," Frankie said. "At this rate we'll be out until midnight."

He put the truck in neutral and rolled us to the lemonade stand. "Should I give them $50 or a full $100?" he asked me.

"Don't give them anything. Their lemonade probably stinks."

"I've been saving this money for a while. I wanted to donate it to a charity."

Frankie leaned out his window and handed $100 to the closest kid. She was little and blonde. Her mouth fell open when she realized what was happening.

"Wowww," the other kid said.

"You guys keep it up, and don't listen to what your parents say," Frankie told them. "It's all about money. If they had worked harder you wouldn't have to be selling lemonade at dawn on a Saturday."

The girl handed him a cup of lemonade. I was too shocked to speak. Once we were out of sight, Frankie took a sip and spit it back out into the cup.

"You were right," he said as he threw the cup out the window. "That little bitch just sold me a cup of yellow Kool-Aid."

CHAPTER SEVEN

Weekly Service #2

1

"The first pool of the day is always the worst," Frankie said. "You're cold and you don't want to be there."

"I'm hot now and I still don't want to be here."

Frankie was so tan from the first pool that his face and his Guinea-tee were morphing into the same shade of sweaty black. I looked at my white skin. I couldn't even remember the last time I had seen the sun.

"Frankie, please stop at the next 7-Eleven," I said. "I need protection."

"I always play it safe now since that last infection. Don't go for the ultra-thins, though. They rip."

I remembered I was wearing the bathing suit that housed his last infection.

"I need sunscreen, not condoms," I said. "I heard they shot missiles through the ozone layer after Nagasaki to let the waste out, and now it looks *worse* than a ripped condom."

A car accident slowed traffic to a stop. Two lawn

care vans had collided head-on at the intersection up ahead. A couple of brown men were standing around the vans. Lighting cigarettes. Laughing.

Another pickup truck was idling next to us. The guy driving rolled his window down and motioned for us to do the same.

"You see that?" he pointed at the accident.

"Yeah," Frankie said.

"More Mexicans taking our jobs."

"They're part of our struggle, man," I said. "Nothing happens on their terms."

He rolled his window back up.

We sat in the gridlock for another minute. I could see the 7-Eleven up ahead. An ambulance tried to weave through traffic but didn't make it very far. No one was moving their car out of its way.

"It's still early," Frankie said. "You can do one more pool and survive."

He turned us off the highway onto a tree-lined road. A comfortable shade fell over the truck. Little straws of light cut through the leaves like hammocks from Heaven. For the first time in days I started to relax, and as the ambulance siren faded behind us, I almost forgot we were in New Jersey.

The road widened and the trees gave way to big open yards. We were entering a land of expensive dirt. A place where good Jersey boys took their fortunes and laundered them deep. If you could fit a couple cows on your yard The State considered you a "farm," and with that title, a decent lawyer could turn the whole property into a tax write-off. Of course, you already had to be a millionaire to afford that kind of land.

Another happy accident that only lined the pockets of the 1%.

As we passed mansion after mansion, I looked at all the fat cows just standing there, chewing on grass. The sun seemed to shine a little brighter. There were weeping cherry trees at the end of long driveways. Their small leaves shone a vibrant pink when the sun attached to them. They danced across front yards as the breeze caught its breath through their branches.

A soft whistle of time not passing.

The sound of revelation.

Between the livestock, the plants, the mowed lawns, I began to think that maybe this day might turn around.

"You know what, Frankie," I said. "This might be all right, after all."

2

"I think I should just take my dog and move into the woods for a while," I said. "Go back to nature."

"Not with the run you're having. Girls come in waves. No telling when the next batch may be."

"They're all the same, though. Except the Queen. I can't stop thinking about her."

I didn't realize it until then, but there *she* was again. I hadn't seen her in years before the 7-Eleven parking lot, and now it seemed impossible to go on without her. We shared each other like we had shared others, and she'd stay for a time. But I knew eventually the wine would get drunk. The ashtrays would fill. We'd move on. People and relationships are so doomed in this America. Life would tell us to bunker down; only experience each other like the last two beating hearts on earth. And someday we would be strangers again. We'd find others to latch onto. It would be just like all the other times only a little more gray. Eventually I'd become another footnote in her story, fading into the dusty pages of a young lover's library.

"Didn't she get tag-teamed behind the dugout junior year?" Frankie asked.

"Yeah."

"Was that Lunchbox she smashed after prom?"

"Yeah."

"Life makes about as much sense as a Maury Povich paternity test."

"I just can't believe she hooked up with Lunchbox. That one bothers me way more."

"Well, it's all in the past, right?"

"Nothing is in the past when you stay in your hometown."

"I guess you've got two choices then. You can deal with it, or you can tell the bitch to take a hike. You already banged her out so I don't really see the point in talking to her anymore."

I had a sudden vision of our seventh-grade hallway. "Dude, I just remembered something I haven't thought about in years. She made me an origami cootie catcher once, back in middle school." I made an algorithm motion with my hands as if they were operating the paper fortune teller. "I asked it if she was the love of my life-time."

"What did it say?"

I scratched my forehead.

"It said, '*Try again*'..."

3

We turned into a new neighborhood called Autumn Hill. There was no hill. There were no trees. There was barely any grass. Building had stopped. A dozen houses sat in varying stages of construction. Pool #2 was in the back-yard of the unfortunate family who had been duped into buying first.

Autumn Hill was on par to look like every other development of New Jersey McMansions. Each house came with a three-car garage no one could ever have enough golf clubs to fill. Kitschy chandeliers would soon hang like melting wedding cakes in the front windows. And the few finished exteriors were a real testament to a class of all appetite and no taste: facades of red brick, which looked great dead-on, but the other three walls were wrapped in ugly vinyl siding. $1,000,000 worth of mortgage, and all you got was a gigantic fugazi and a brown lawn you'd spend every summer trying to bring back to life.

"This is some mess," I said. "Nobody else is moving in here. These poor people won't get half of their money back if they sell now."

"Which means they're never going to pay."

"Let's loosen the bolts on the diving board. Then when the kids jump on it … BAM."

He looked at me like he was ready to send me to the gallows. "I always knew there was something wrong with you. But my God, that's just sickening."

"Whatever. Let's get this junk unloaded fast. If I don't have more coffee soon I'm going to become a real asshole."

We were pulling things out of the truck bed when we heard a car horn coming up the street. It bled into a continuous beep and pierced our ears like a demon call.

"It sounds like the Gestapo is coming to get us," I said.

Frankie had his hands locked around the crate of chemicals. He dropped it, said, "I just can't take it anymore," and climbed up on the bed and reached through the rear window into the truck. His hand came back holding a two-foot metal pole. Then he said, "Yee-haw, Londi!" and did a running jump off the bed and took off toward the horn.

A white Chevy Express van rolled by. It had a blue **Pool Universe** decal across its side door. Two guys in matching blue polo shirts were hanging out the window, giving Frankie the finger.

I grabbed a bag of shock and followed Frankie down the street. He was transforming into Frankie Gunnz right before my eyes. His muscles bulged. Veins rose. Like a beast with its balls tied, an electric fence couldn't restrain him.

The Pool Universe van stopped short every fifteen feet in front of Frankie. He'd start to turn around, to take the high road, but they laughed and called him a pussy until he started chasing again.

Then he kicked off his flip flops and almost caught them barefoot.

"You bastards!" he said. "Find your mothers and kiss them goodbye."

I caught up with him and launched the bag of shock as they sped off for good. It landed with a dull *thunk* twenty feet away on the street.

Frankie looked at me with his eyebrows quivering. "What did I tell you about wasting chemicals?"

I picked up the bag of shock and apologized.

4

The pool didn't even have one worm sliding around its concrete floor. A crawling Aquabot vacuum had done our job for us. It was a purple machine the size of a Tonka Truck that drove around the pool and ate everything.

Frankie pointed at it. "These robots are going to re-place me soon. It's already made the pool spotless."

I thought this meant we could leave, but Frankie said we had to look like we were doing some for *at least* forty-five minutes.

"They bought the ticket," he said about the home-owners. "They get the show."

I set the pump up but I couldn't find an outlet to plug it into. I stood there with the cord in my hand while Frankie did a set of sit ups.

"Follow the bees," he said. "They're always building nests in the outdoor outlets."

I had started to notice a steady code when it came to tricks of the pool trade - use nature against itself.

Frankie still had some coffee left from our breakfast at Dunkin' Donuts. We poured the rest of his cup along the back patio. Then we waited.

A single bee appeared. It flew over us and buzzed down on a fun noodle floating in the pool.

"This is taking forever," Frankie said. "There must be a honey buffet around here."

"Even the bees think Dunkin' Donuts sucks."

But then I thought of a way to earn my lunch. I roll-ed my arm around the coffee puddle until it was nice and sticky, then I held it up in the air, hoping the wind would spread my stink around like something that needed poll-inating.

A hornet showed up and landed on my arm. I don't know what I was expecting to happen, but I didn't like it when it did.

I stuck my tongue out in disgust.

"Don't move," Frankie whispered. "It's working."

The hornet lifted off. It hovered for a few seconds,

then sailed around the corner of the house.

"Now what?" I asked.

"We track it."

Frankie picked up the two-foot metal pole he'd chased the Pool Universe van with. Black electrical tape had been wrapped around the handle for better grip.

"Why do you keep this pole with you?" I asked.

"I named her Black Beauty, bro." He held the pole out so I could get a good look at the handle. "I made her into the perfect killing tool."

"What's it for?"

"It's called a safety pole. It's how you get a pool cover off the grommets that hold it through winter." He smacked the pole against his open palm. "And you can bang it off someone's head with a quick swing."

We turned the corner and saw a black cloud of bees. They were circling an outlet like a tornado of thirsty needles.

"Ok, I've got a plan," Frankie said. "You go pop the case around the outlet open. Then run away as fast as you can."

"That sounds like suicide. What are you going to do?"

"I'll cover you." He choked up on the safety pole. "I'm a samurai with this thing."

I made it to the outlet without getting stung, but the bees started diving at me as soon as I touched the case. Frankie grabbed my neck and told me to run. Then he shouted at the bees like a cop in a riot: "BACK DOWN MOTHERFUCKERS! BACK DOWN!" I could hear wind rushing around his pole as he swung it. If he missed just once the pack would swallow him whole.

I put half the backyard between us before I turned around. Frankie was jumping like a mad man, swatting at the hovering bees.

After he'd beaten the last one to death he called me over. Bee corpses lay on their backs, staring at the sun. Curious grackles started yelling at each other from the bushes. They were drooling over the bee slaughter like someone had spilled a bag of potato chips.

I plugged the pump in while Frankie counted dead bees. "Do you think this will hurt my karma?" he asked.

"Nah. It was us or them."

"I hope you're right."

"Wake and bake?"

"Yeah," he didn't sound so sure. "Wake and bake."

We sat at the edge of the pool and relaxed for a minute. I pulled the pipe out of my pocket and we took a few drags.

"What kind of scumbags drive the Pool Universe van?" I asked.

"The worst kind. They do Bon Jovi's pool on the Navesink River. They have a monopoly on all the mansions out there."

"What are they doing around here?"

"I don't know, bro. That's what we're going to find out."

5

There was nothing to do at the house, but in case anyone drove by and double-checked, the alibi of grueling labor needed to check out. That's the way work goes, from the boss down to any asshole with a checkbook. No one ever knows what you are up to, but they will pay you so long as they think you are miserable while doing it.

We threw tools around the concrete of the pool. Frankie turned the pump on for some noise. Then we got another safety pole from the truck and headed out for a recon mission around the neighborhood.

The street had just been paved. We could see dotted reflections of fresh radiator fluid shining green on the new asphalt. Frankie kneeled at one of the stains. He tapped it with his pinky, then rubbed it on his tongue.

"Spoiled Pool Universe bitches," he growled, his face reddening under all of that Sicilian sweat. "Real pool boys never use the air conditioner during pool season. They sweat it out. Like men."

We followed the drips over a main road into another development. It looked exactly like Autumn Hill, only this one had a sign that said: Autumn Field.

The Pool Universe van was parked in front of the first McMansion, taunting us like the Cheshire Cat.

"There it is, Frankie! You've got the instincts of a bloodhound."

"Londi," he said, "sometimes you get exactly what you deserve."

I'd never been involved in a rivalry of this nature. A real classic sort of American grudge, like the Hatfields and McCoys. Nobody certain of how it started, but all the outlaws understood their sacred duty. Frankie's younger brother was approaching working age and it didn't look like a truce was in the works. If Bon Jovi was going to keep giving his royalties to Pool Universe we'd have to deal with them the old-fashioned way. Otherwise, Frankie's brother would soon be working for American Pools. And from Memorial through Labor he'd be out on these lonely roads, inheriting an oath to vengeance that began long before most of these backyards traded their trees for pools.

We crouched behind a bush and caught our breath. The Pool Universe van looked right at home in the land of the gilded. The McMansion it was parked in front of had a gate on a track that opened up to a long driveway. You almost had to appreciate the bourgeoisie commitment to distinguishing themselves from the minions - slaving for them wasn't enough; they had to make you park in the street and march first.

The backyard was walled off from the road by a massive fence of bamboo. It was perfect for camouflage. We crawled through the brush like tunnel rats, ready to make an ambush.

Frankie put his index finger against his lips. I nodded back. Then we poked our heads through the bamboo line and saw two young kids skimming the pool.

"Look at those happy twerps," Frankie said. "Not a worry in the world. Their whole lives ahead of them."

Their blue polo shirts had the company name stitched across the chest. The shirts were ironed and tucked into tan cargo shorts. And their flip flops weren't like ours; they looked like some intern spent all night shining them with spit and a horsehair brush.

"What kind of lame-ass charade is this?" I asked. "Their uniforms cost more than our truck. I bet Bon Jovi owns the company."

"Come on," Frankie said. "Let's go."

"Go? We have to beat them silly with our safety poles."

"No, bro. I cooled down. We just have to let it go."

"We could at least rob their van."

He looked down at the ground and seemed to be tallying up offenses. "Yeah. Okay. That seems fair."

He stood guard.

The front doors were locked but they'd left the back open. I climbed in and saw how the other half lived. Shelves and pole clips were installed throughout the interior like a mobile pool store. In very neatly arranged boxes, every tool, plug, screw, and chemical was properly labeled. I'd never heard of the company before an hour ago, but they had gotten themselves to the top of a long list of things I wanted to hurt in record time.

I checked the cabin for contraband. No weed hidden in the usual places. No booze either. All I saw were gluten-free granola bars. No good. Not on a day like this. I wanted to eat real food - something fried that used to walk on all fours.

I found a Zippo lighter under the driver's seat. It was engraved with the Soviet hammer and sickle. I put it in my pocket and looked for something I could subtly destroy.

A bucket of D.E. sat innocently between the two front seats. I unscrewed the lid but left it carefully placed on the bucket. This way, when they hit a bump, the D.E. powder would explode all over the van like a flour bomb.

I showed Frankie the Zippo but didn't mention the D.E. explosive I had planted. He would either find it genius or deplorable on every level. You could never tell with him.

He traced the hammer and sickle with his thumbnail and said, "Those butt-sniffing pinkos. I understand hating the competition, but to hate freedom ... what kind of apostates are we dealing with?"

"Total traitors. We should have drowned and buried them when we had the chance."

"If I had known where their loyalties lie then, I would have."

We walked back to our house on Autumn Hill feeling like we had let America down.

CHAPTER EIGHT

1

I was saving a victory cigarette for the drive away from the pool. I was trying to prolong it so I had something to look forward to. Plus, I had the ultimate fire tool now: a lighter used on mountains people wrote books about climbing. A lighter that never jammed in war trenches where soot rained down on soldiers like a dirty snow. The novelty of using a Zippo to light a cigarette was like mom's homemade sauce over a plate of macaroni.

Frankie filled out the bill while I collected the junk we'd thrown around the pool. No one ever showed up or peered over the fence.

We were home free.

"Let's hope we get five more of these," I said.

"Don't count on it, bro. Our next pool is an opening, and the Boss is sending extra help."

"What have these people been waiting for? We're halfway through May."

"I know. That's what scares me."

2

I spun the wheel of the Zippo and got nothing but a spark. Even Communism is against me, I thought. I spun it again and again. Each time, a little cloud of black smoke fumed out.

"Stop, bro," Frankie said. "You're going to break the flint."

"Half-assed American machinery. We used to fly to the moon. Now we can't even build a lighter?"

"That's not a real Zippo. It probably says *Made In China* on the bottom."

"I'll bet they've got a whole team of kids in some basement putting these things together. They're selling our own history right back to us."

"It's a worldwide conspiracy for sure. We're just scratching the surface."

Somehow it was 10:00 a.m. Everything made the world smell like a big rotting corpse. The coffee crash had come and gone. I felt like a rented mule.

"Frankie, I have to eat. If I smoke another cigarette without more food, I'm going to puke."

"One more pool. Then we'll eat."

We stopped at a gas station to fill up, then headed back toward our hometown. It was a decent hike. Frankie and I just stared through the dirty windshield. There was nothing left to talk about worth the effort of conversation.

I saw an old woman sitting on a porch swing with a bowl of popcorn. I watched kids on bicycles. I used to have one of those, I thought. I went everywhere on it. To my friends' houses. To Queen Jac's house when we were both so young we just wanted to chase frogs. And we did. We spent hours in creeks chasing frogs until her mother came screaming for her and we were covered in slime. I had everything I wanted. It was simple.

Why did we hand over our youth so easily? Now I had to work all day so I could get enough money to bring her to the bar. To get her back where I'd had her in the first place. I don't even own a bicycle anymore. I'm sure my joints are too stiff to bend over and catch frogs. The days pass in a fast wave now, and the nights bring *real* terror. They keep me on my knees like the sad and praying nuns; attempting some dharmic exercise to accept everything on earth. So I drink, and once in a while I remember I'm a man. Those are the nights I step into the ring and box up a weight class. And sometimes, under the right bar lights, it's exactly what a Queen is looking for.

"What do you think death feels like?" I asked Frankie.

He thought for a minute. "Paralyzed glue?"

"That must feel better than sleep."

"I'll bet it does."

"Sounds pretty good, Frankie. I'm going to drown myself in the next pool."

I reached my head out the window, hocked back, and spit a black rock of mucus out into the air.

Yes. It was time to die.

CHAPTER NINE

1

The Boss called Frankie. It sounded like the next pool was in terrible shape. Frankie said "okay" a couple of times and then hung the phone out the window while the Boss continued yapping. He looked at me and made the motion of slitting his throat. Then he handed me the phone and said, "Just hang up whenever he shuts up."

I clicked 'end' and dropped the phone on the seat.

"We need to find a Home Depot," Frankie said.

"We need to boycott those evil thugs before they put everyone out of business."

"They already did. There's nowhere else to go."

"We can't sellout now. We have all the momentum. Get the internet up on your phone. I'll start a group."

"There's a diner around the corner. Will you shut up if I get you some food?"

"Definitely."

2

The two hottest women in New Jersey were standing

outside of the diner holding clipboards. They were both wearing white lab coats altered at the waist into hourglass-shaped skirts. Then long, tanned legs all the way down to high heels. The uniform made them look like time travelers. Or members of a suicide cult.

"Holy cow, bro," Frankie said. "Look at the funbags on those broads."

Every time someone walked into the diner the girls smiled at them and tried to pass off a heap of papers. This kind of harassment went against everything pure and sacred in our great country, but after one look at them I wanted to hand over the Boss' debit card and follow them anywhere.

We got out of the truck and their high heels clicked right over. They could really move in those things. Like two Pleiadian angels floating over the parking lot at us. Blonde hair. Blue eyes you could stand up and dive into.

"I'm Adina," the one closest to me said. "And this is Haushinka. We're members of The Church of Dianetics."

We all shook hands. Frankie kissed the back of Adina's like he was Prince Charming.

"Do you have a few minutes to take a survey?" Haushinka asked us.

Frankie winked at her. "How could anyone say 'no' to you two?"

They led us to a corner booth in the diner. Full clipboards were already waiting for us on the table. They held in-depth survey questions, about thirty sheets of paper deep.

I turned each one and scanned up and down. I must've been making a face because when Haushinka handed me a pen she said, "Just be honest."

There was something so warming in her eyes. The

way you catch your mother looking at you sometimes when you lose too much faith in the world. Some inner quality all women possess that promises, "It's going to be okay."

"This is retarded," Frankie said. He took our clipboards and handed them over. "We've got work to do, ladies."

I grabbed one.

"I'll hang on to mine," I said to Haushinka. "Maybe I can find you when I'm done."

She smiled at me and gave me a business card. I looked for her number, but the only contact was: *info @infoscientology.com.*

They said goodbye and went back outside.

"Frankie, we blew it."

"Puh-lease. I knew right away those babes weren't going to give it up."

I started checking boxes on the survey and a waitress came over. "Sorry about them," she said. "I'd chase them away, but honestly, I'm afraid of them. They say they're with a church, but I think they're Scientologists."

We said it was fine and she told us we had hit the brunch special. Everything came with free mimosas.

"Mimosas?" Frankie said. "Do we look like we're on a date over here?"

"He wishes," I said to the waitress. "We'll take eggs and a dozen mimosas."

"We're working," Frankie reminded me. "We'll take one mimosa each."

I filled out the last page of the survey. I knew it was looking bad even before I tallied up my answers. The question, "*Do people often regret asking for your opinion?*" particularly bothered me.

The waitress put two glasses full of yellow juice on

our table. Frankie became concerned when I didn't reach for mine.

"What does the survey say?" he asked.

"It says I'm beyond-help depressed. Jesus, I'm going to kill myself."

"What?"

"I knew I was sad, but I really think I might die."

Frankie read through a couple of the pages. "What a bunch of shit."

"Frankie, I need help."

He raised his hand at the waitress and motioned for two more. "Shut up and drink, bro."

"I'd kill myself right now if I could start over. Honest. I've never told anyone that."

"You're not depressed."

"You think I'm all right?"

He crumbled up the pages and looked at his phone. "No, I don't think you're all right. But I think you're too stupid to kill yourself."

He threw some money at me and said he was going to call the Boss.

The waitress brought two more mimosas over and put them next to the others. I told her to forget about our food and sit down and drink one of the mimosas. She sat down across from me and chugged a glass. I stuck straws in the other three and took a few gulps.

"Almost done with your shift?" I said after a hiccup.

"Not even close."

"I guess it never really ends, does it?"

"No," she zoned out into her empty glass. "Not for us."

A litany of uzi-speed Spanish came through the kitchen doors from a few different male voices. Then our peace was killed by plates or bowls breaking against the floor like ceramic projectiles.

I saw a line form on her forehead that looked more like a scar than a wrinkle. "Are you the one who has to handle that?"

"Of course," she said. "I'm covering for the manager."

"I think you should wait a few minutes before you go in there. Give them a chance to kill each other first."

She reached for my hand and laid her face on the table. I held it and counted gray hairs swimming away from the back of her head.

"How much does covering for the manager pay?" I asked.

"It pays me $2.15 an hour. Plus tips."

"We're living in history's dumbest plague."

She rubbed her thumb around the back of my hand. Then she lifted her head from the table and asked, "Do you mind if we do this just a little longer?"

I didn't even answer. We just sat there silently in a stalemate of safety, like we were trading plasma or Christmas morning through our palms. A whole world collapsing around us but together we had found a blank postcard, and our touch was the first step in writing a letter back to God.

We talked endlessly in that silence.

It was the best conversation I've ever had.

3

I went outside eventually and found Frankie sitting in our truck.

"Whoever the Boss is sending to help with the next pool got caught up," he said. "They need us to wait an hour."

"An hour? I'm never going to see the Queen again."

"I have a date tomorrow night. I'm going to get a mani-pedi next door." He pointed at his feet. "And little tiny fish are going to clean my toes."

4

The diner was in one of those strip mall things. Next to a puppy store, a nail salon, an out-of-business music shop, and a Dunkin' Donuts.

I smoked a cigarette outside of the nail salon. I could see Frankie through the front window. Two Chinese ladies were using a popsicle stick to rub wax above and below his eyebrows.

I curled my lip in confusion. Frankie pointed at me and laughed. Both ladies laughed. Frankie closed his eyes and made a slow air-humping motion.

I went inside and they sat Frankie in a chair.

"I forgot to ask, bro," he said. "Do you want to get waxed?"

"No."

One of the women popped her hands open around a poster like I'd won a prize. It was a picture of a big ass in a neon bathing suit. Long strands of pubes came out from under the bathing suit like the tentacles of a colossal squid. The bottom of the poster had "Brazilian Wax" written in pink text.

"Half-price," she said to me.

Everyone laughed again. Except me.

Frankie reclined his chair and they placed his feet into a tub. Then they poured a fish tank full of tiny guppies over his feet.

Frankie put on a big dumb grin. "I didn't think they would tickle so much."

"That's fucking disgusting," I said.

All three of them stopped and looked at me.

"HEY," Frankie said. "Watch your language. There are women here."

I sat down. A plate full of mud splattered out from under my butt. I jumped up, thinking I'd sat on a fish.

I rubbed my hand across the mess and came up with a blob of wax.

"Oh no," both women said. "Very bad. Very bad."

They came over and took off my shirt. They started to take off my shorts.

"Whoa," I said. "Don't take off my shorts."

"We clean."

"I don't have any other clothes."

They got my shorts off. I stood there with my hands cupped around my junk, trying to keep everything tucked in. Frankie was laughing so hard he was kicking guppies out of the tub. I didn't turn around, but I knew everyone driving by could see my bare ass through the front window.

One of the women threw a bathrobe at me. I had to make a choice: I could catch it and expose myself for a second, or I could let it fall and bend over.

5

Every kid in the county was outside of Home Depot wearing a uniform. Baseball jerseys. Soccer jerseys. All begging for money to burn on their inane teams. It was fundraiser season, another chance for everyone to rob each other in the spirit of children.

The fat parents sat in chairs and guarded the money. Boys tossed baseballs back and forth. A bunch of bald kids in wheelchairs made it impossible for the suckers to ignore their donation jars. The sounds of their collective happiness made me hate them. It was like listening to a thousand weak animals being skinned alive.

The Girl Scouts ran the whole show. It was probably legacy. No major scandals had forced them into the corners like the Boy Scouts. The other groups could be avoided, but not the Girl Scouts. Their long table was right in front of the entrance to Home Depot.

A few mothers circled the Girl Scouts camp like caged tigers. Their hair up in messy buns. The same high heels as the Scientologists but nothing sexy about their strut. They had been girls once, with enough of *something* to get a man on one knee. I watched them teach their daughters how to hustle, how to make someone's money slip away.

Some poor guy in white socks and flip flops got out of his car. I could see in his step he had just finished a long week. A hawk-eyed mother whispered into her daughter's ear. The girls watched until the guy got close. Then, as a flock, they swarmed him like hungry gnats.

They got everything but his socks.

"Too bad I wasted so much money on that crappy lemonade," Frankie said. "I wish I could give all these kids something."

I looked at the Girl Scouts, then at my robe.

"I'm going to wait in the truck," I said.

"Why?"

"I'm pretty sure it's a crime to go into a store wearing a bathrobe."

"I don't think sitting in a parking lot watching Girl Scouts would play any better."

I got out of the truck. "Let's make it quick."

Frankie stopped at the Girl Scouts table to buy a box of Thin Mints. The girls tried to hit me with a sales pitch but I ignored them and went into the Home Depot. A breeze came through the door with me. The orchids were on display, swaying back and forth in the wind like peacock feathers. Beautiful orchids. Purple. Pink. Heaven white. My mother would have gone mad for each one.

Frankie came into the store and showed me the Thin Mints. "Do you want one?"

"No."

He dropped the box into a garbage can. "I don't know what I was thinking. I'm trying to watch my figure."

The place was full of men hunched over from years of honest work. We walked to the plumbing aisle and passed dozens of them in cut-off t-shirts. Shirts for roofing companies. For painting companies. They coughed at each other in the same language, some acknowledgement that they'd finally made it to the weekend, and for two days they could stop fixing other people's homes and finally look at their own.

Frankie started pulling random PVC pipes off the shelf and inspecting them.

"How am I supposed to know what's what?" he said. "They don't label anything."

"Go ask someone."

"Nobody in any of these goddamn stores knows anything. I'm going to make it my life goal to put these SON-OF-A-BITCH deadbeats out of business."

I picked up a copy of *The Farmer's Almanac*. The forecast called for a mild summer. A few tips for baking a Blue Ribbon pie. The horoscopes - all positive predictions. Where was this wonderful America?

"What does today's horoscope say?" Frankie asked. Then he just pulled the book out of my hand and mouthed each day until he got to May 15th. "I knew it. Ruled by Taurus. We're screwed."

He said it was bad. He studied the PVC and said *that* was bad.

A guy in a uniform walked by our aisle. He did a double take of my bathrobe and stopped.

"We've been made," I said. "They're going to call the cops on me."

Frankie reached back over his head and pulled his shirt off like a hockey player. "Let them call the cops on me too."

The uniform kept looking.

"He thinks your eyebrows are hot," I said.

"Shut up."

"Wake and bake?"

Frankie threw the almanac back onto the shelf. I lifted my fist and he punched it.

"Fuck Home Depot," he said. "Let's go get your clothes back."

6

The Scientologists were gone. In the handicap spot, a family of five sat in lawn chairs. The father had his pants strapped up around his chest by suspenders. His wife wore a bucket hat covered with Ron Paul pins.

"Here we go again," Frankie said. "Don't sign anything."

The yellow *"Don't Tread On Me"* flag flew proudly over their camp, but I had a feeling it wasn't taxation without representation they were out protesting. The flag looked hijacked waving above their heads, like a Che Guevara poster on sale at the mall.

The father was too fat to move. He grabbed one of

his sons by the shoulder and pushed him at us. The kid bounced over with a big corn-fed smile. The whole promise of democracy and civil action evident in every freckle on his face.

"Tell them the part about the bailout," the father shouted.

The kid had the whole spiel ready for us. "Hey patriots," he said. "Do you think it's time to restore The Constitution?"

He handed us a leaflet that said: **RESTORE THE CONSTITUTION. WE NEED A RON PAUL REVOLUTION!** A little Tea Party stamp sat in the corner like some eye of the Illuminati.

"You can forget about The Constitution," Frankie said. "Money won."

I was looking at a child who had never known a world before 9/11. His whole existence would revolve around pushing a button on a phone. Everything made safe for the children. Anything kooky or kinky had already been banned and forgotten. That eagle at the end of the flagpole would never mean a thing to him.

And here he was, trying to restore a lost world his father believed could come back.

"This is the most important lesson you need to learn," I said to him. "You can do anything before you turn sixteen. You want to throw rocks at cops? Do it. You want to blow up an ATM? Do it."

"That's not enough," he said. "I want to save the world."

Where does this sense of duty come from? I was a little kid once who shit when I wanted and slept just as easy. I was going to save the world, too. I felt it. And twenty years later I crawl through my days with my eyes half open, wondering why my back hurts all the time. I know bartenders better than my friends. I drive down parkways that turn into turnpikes with a song playing that says the same thing, not sure where I'm going. And suddenly I get there, not remembering anything I've passed. Like there's a destination I'm headed toward beyond the sun where my soul won't be lost. Something that no one would buy but it's all I've got to sell. Maybe I make it there. But then what? What's good enough to stop a man from moving?

"You really want to save the world?" I asked him. "Then go give your mother a hug. She's the only thing that matters."

The kid took the leaflet back and walked to his father. I could tell he was repeating our advice.

"We better go," I said to Frankie. "Libertarians love the 2nd Amendment."

I watched the kid sit in his chair and give his father a suspicious look. I wondered if we had just taken the last smile he would ever give.

7

We walked into the salon and Haushinka was lying face down on the waxing table. Her clothes were in a pile on the floor. A towel covered the smooth curve of her lower back.

"Hey you," she looked up at me. "How'd you do on the survey?"

"I think I failed."

One of the Chinese women was steaming my clothes against the wall. The other had her head buried in Haushinka's backside, applying something. Haushinka reached back and spread her cheeks apart while she told me about the power of therapy.

"To be a fly on this wall," Frankie whispered to me.

The lady studied Haushinka's landscape like the lost truth of the Universe was hidden in there. Then she gave her a little pat and said, "Ready?"

"Let's do it," Haushinka said to her. "Make it count."

"Okay. On three. One. Two ..."

On three she reached between Haushinka's legs and we heard a violent tear. Her hand jerked back with a sheet of waxing tape stuck to her fingers. It was covered in a tuft of black hair like she had just pulled a skunk out of Haushinka's ass.

Haushinka didn't even blink.

"Yuck," I said.

Frankie stood on his tiptoes and analyzed Haushinka's waxed turf. "Nice work," he said to the lady. "Do you guys do rub-and-tugs too?"

She held the hairy tape and said, "Of course. And 10th one is free!"

"Then listen up, toots. I've got a date tomorrow. If it doesn't work out I'm coming back for you." He turned around and pointed at the one steaming my clothes. "Or you."

She put the steamer down and brought my clothes over on a hanger. The other followed, with the tape still in hand. "Runaround Sue" came on the radio and they both started swinging their hips in a coordinated dance that looked like *The Twist*.

The one with the tape did a spin and the tape grazed my face. Little bristles of hair tickled my lips. The other handed me a card. Good for a free tan.

"What's this for?" I asked her.

She pointed right at my groin.

"No good," she said. "Need tan."

CHAPTER TEN

The Opening

1

The rich acres of western Monmouth County were behind us. The only cows we'd be seeing now would be sandwiched between two pieces of bread. From here on out it was blue-collar turf all the way, until the fence of the almighty Atlantic separated us from Europe's sandy shores. A ripe spot of the American experiment. All the jobs were pointless and nothing weird was accepted. Parents sent their boys to the unions and made their daughters teach third grade. Any kid who wouldn't comply was shipped to Brooklyn.

For whatever reason, paying to maintain a pool for three months a year was a justified expense. A pool and a new TV; the only things the middle-class felt right investing in between vacations to Disney World.

We turned into a neighborhood and all the streets were named after trees. What a sick game of doublespeak, I thought. They obliterate nature and then they pretend to memorialize it.

"I haven't been to this pool in a few years," Frankie said. "It's always a mess."

An Old Bridge police car was sitting in the driveway when we pulled up to the house.

"Crap. Hide the weed," Frankie pointed at the police car. "I didn't know the Boss was sending Ralph to help."

"Is this the same Ralph the Boss was talking shit about earlier?"

"Yeah. He's so useless we should get a bonus for working with him."

"I didn't know Ralph was a cop."

"How else could he get away with being such a moron?"

"Why did he bring his police car?"

"The town pays for his gas."

"Well, I guess it's good to have a cop on our side. I can expose that guy Carl from the gas station before he robs another hard-working citizen."

Ralph stepped out of his car and did a stretch like he had just woken up from a coma. I tried to fan away some of the weed stink before he got close, but that never worked with cops.

He stuck his head in Frankie's window and didn't seem to notice the smell. His wrinkles formed a deep V that came down between his eyebrows and the bridge of his nose. It gave his face a look of permanent anger.

"We've got a real piece of shit on our hands here, Frankie," he said.

Frankie tried to introduce us but the rotten bastard paid no mind. He took off his sunglasses and squinted like he was trying to read something far away. The same albino-raccoon tan that the Boss had was printed on his face as well.

"I did the lay of the land already," Ralph continued.

"It's a shipwreck back there, about ready to go down."

"Listen, Officer," I started, "there's this maniac named Carl, he pretends to man a gas pump, he's fluent in at least two languages ..."

Ralph interrupted me with a burp, so deep from his stomach's pit, that the rearview mirror actually vibrated. He was obviously drunk as hell and trying to focus, but his pupils danced around his eyes like rubber marbles.

He didn't say anything else. He just walked to the street and spit at it a couple times while Frankie and I unloaded the equipment.

I looked into the back of Ralph's cop car. There was an empty thirty of Budweiser on the backseat. And another thirty of Bud Light that had been cracked into.

"Frankie," I said, "this guy is drunker than rush week at Rutgers. You can't let a customer see him like this."

"Not our problem, bro. He's the Boss' brother-in-law. Let him deal with it."

I shrugged at the strange hierarchy we all abided by. But maybe I was letting Ralph's bad reputation shape my opinion of him. After all, he was a fine-looking cop. His tribal tattoos spiraled up and down arms solid as oak trees. And when the light caught him just right he looked almost like an old Viking. But he had been broken before his golden years and he seemed to know it. His face showed the scars of at least one bad divorce. And if he had ever walked with a purpose no one remembered or cared. He was a lame animal bumbling around with a stomach full of cheap beer now, relying completely on a badge and bloodline to repay the debts this lifestyle inevitably accrued.

I wasn't mad that Ralph didn't help with the load. But it did make me more confident when I asked him for a beer.

2

I waited until Frankie went to the backyard before hitting Ralph up for a Bud Light. He was a smart guy as far as cops go. For one, he knew that with a limited supply of beer we needed to optimize the alcohol.

"Let's shotgun these bitches," Ralph said.

We hid behind the truck and shotgunned our cans.

After Ralph burped most of the alphabet, he asked, "You got a girlfriend?"

"I don't know."

"Kid, you either do or you don't. I catch my son up in his room with a different girl every week. He doesn't know anything either."

"I'm in love. I think."

"Don't say that. How long have you known her?"

"Since sixth grade."

"Have you fucked her yet?"

"Yeah."

"How'd she do?"

"I can't remember. I don't care. I just want to hold her and cry forever."

"You all talk like you've been through it. Like you were strung up and beaten front and back. Wait for your third divorce."

"She's the one. I know it."

Deep shadows fit like puzzle pieces between his wrinkles. They disappeared as he scowled in thought, then suddenly opened up like big black voids when he was ready to speak.

"You're playing the Devil this time," he said.

"What do you mean?"

"My Grandpa used to say it. He fell in love with some French whore during the war."

"My girl is Cuban, I think."

"He meant it as a warning. That the girl you're in love with is never the one you end up with."

"It's got to work out for somebody."

"You're a man. If you found some floozy to lie around with and talk about sunsets forever, you'd never get anything done."

"What does the Devil have to do with it?"

"He's in your woman. You love someone like that you'll drink the poison. You'll get your ass kicked in every bar."

"I've lost fights for less."

"I know. You're going to do it anyway. Just remember, they're all the same. She'll have you screaming in the street eventually."

I wasn't sure if we had reached an agreement. He was probably right but I didn't care. I kicked our empty cans and thought about my father: "You always have to learn everything the hard way," was one of his favorites.

"Oh, hell," Ralph belched. "Might as well do another. This is gonna suck."

I wasn't going to argue. He handed me a beer. We did another. Ralph threw up a pile of foam onto the tire well of our truck.

"No matter how bad life gets make sure you stick with beer, kid," he said while wiping his mouth. "You can be an alcoholic forever as long as you drink beer. You just piss out the poison."

3

The three of us stood at the edge of the mesh pool cover, stretched like skin being sewn back to a bone. From corner to corner. Grommet to grommet. The infomercial claimed that the cover could hold an elephant. And maybe ten years ago it could've done just that. But a decade of winters is a long time. Entire squares were missing. And heaps of what looked like dead animals were clumped together on the cover, baked into the worn scraps of canvas.

"I'm going to grab the rest of the beer," Ralph announced to no one. "It's even worse than I remember."

About halfway back, a waterfall had been chiseled from a big mound of concrete. An extended piece of slate stuck out of it and reached over the pool. I pictured a dawn sun hitting the water spilling from the slate and the rainbow that the reflection would cause. But was that even beautiful? I couldn't decide if artificial rainbows were anything special.

The waterfall was a real pain because of how it sloped down to the edge of the pool. There was no way to reach the grommet drilled into its base without hanging off of it. I looked down at a series of crisscrossing latches holding the cover to the side. Somehow an inventive pool boy had buckled it all together.

Frankie circled the pool like an angry goose. He lit another cigarette off the one he was smoking. Then he stopped and stared at the waterfall for a long time.

He didn't have to say it. I knew we were in over our heads on this one.

"This cover obviously can't be used again," he sighed. "That's the only good news I have."

This meant we wouldn't have to power wash the cover before folding it up and putting it in a bag. It would shave about twenty minutes off the opening, so long as everything else stayed on course.

Frankie told me to get a safety pole as he went to the other side of the pool with Black Beauty.

"How are we supposed to get the cover loose under the waterfall?" I asked him.

"I haven't figured that out yet."

Ralph walked back into the yard with the thirty of Bud Light. "All right, Frankie," he said. "I'm going to deal with that filter."

The filter sat half-hidden behind a row of short bushes. A rusted box stuck out of the ground next to it. "There's a computer in there that controls the whole pool," Frankie said about the box. "But it gets rained on all year and never works."

Ralph dragged the case of beer and a bag of tools behind the bushes. He picked a can and opened it with his teeth. Foam sprayed his face and he lifted the beer slowly away as it drained into his mouth. Like an ugly fat fountain. Then he spiked the empty can against the ground.

"Let me know if anyone comes out," he said to us. "I've got to take a mean piss."

I could hear his urine ricocheting off the bushes while Frankie and I popped the pool cover from the grommets. Once there was some slack, most of the cover sunk a few inches into the water. I hung onto Frankie's shirt while he bent around the waterfall and tried to reach the last grommet. So much sweat poured out of his shirt while I squeezed it was like ringing out a towel.

I heard a loud *ding* and the ring latch slid up his safety pole, over the grommet. "Nailed it," he said. "Nobody's better."

The cover was totally unhooked, but it didn't sink any deeper into the water. Entire sections were being pushed up by some unseen force.

Frankie pulled up a corner so we could get a look underneath.

"Holy moly," I said. "There are trees growing in there."

He let go of the cover and pointed at one of the muck piles we'd thought was a rotting animal. "Those aren't dead animals on the cover. Swamp plants are ripping their way out of the pool!"

The water looked more like the Everglades than a pool. We guessed that through some demented form of photosynthesis, alien-seeds had landed in the water and hatched. The sun's reflection through the pool cover grew the spores like a mutating virus. In these first few weeks of spring an underwater forest had planted and fertilized itself. And now that they had a taste for the sun, the tree limbs broke through the weak mesh cover like they were opening a window for breakfast.

"I've never seen anything like this," Frankie kept saying.

"Sometimes hurricanes scoop up birds on one end and spit them out on the other," I offered. "Maybe that's how this nightmare began."

"The next hurricane better drop off some parrots then ... instead of all these bullshit plants."

We each took a side and pulled the cover toward us onto the yard, folding it over itself every foot and a half. It kept snagging on the tree limbs, so Frankie balanced at the edge of the pool and hacked at them with a safety pole. Green slime spewed as they cracked to pieces and submitted back under the water line.

After we had the last corner folded up, Frankie sat down on the cover and said, "Fuck this whole world."

"Now what?" I asked.

"I'm going to take a piss."

"I have to piss too."

"Then follow me."

We went behind the bushes next to Ralph. He was passed out and snoring against the filter box like only a man with a guaranteed pension could.

Frankie got down on his knees and said, "You have to do it like this." His head was about a foot above the bushes. "This way if anyone walks out," he continued, "it just looks like you're working."

I knelt a few feet away and pissed out all the beer. Frankie whistled "Home On The Range" with a soft vibrato and no sense of irony.

I finished before him and headed back toward the pool. As I was passing the back door an old man came outside. "How long until I can use this goddamn pool?" he asked me.

"I'm not sure. I guess it depends on your constitution."

He had a big bald head. His fingers repeatedly dragged from one side of his scalp to the other as if they were parting hair. "Constitution? I ate people in Korea. Now my grandkids bitch when the air conditioner breaks."

"I'd probably eat a person before I ate a dog."

He stopped rubbing his head in mid-motion and appeared to be weighing the pros and cons of choke-slamming me. "No, you wouldn't. Where the hell is Frankie?"

I had been speaking loudly so Frankie would hear me and know to hurry up. His head emerged from the piss spot and he gave a loud grunt, then he walked over.

"Oh my God," the old man said to Frankie. "The worst mistake I ever made was getting this pool."

That's what everyone must say, I thought.

"Every year it looks like this," he continued. "And every year I swear I'm just going to fill it in with dirt."

I could see from Frankie's wincing eyes that something was wrong, but he kept it cool until the old man went inside.

"Bro," he said to me, "I had to cut the piss short. It feels like a knife is stabbing my gut."

"Frankie, you can't stop mid-stream! That is the number one rule of pissing. You'll never get a boner again."

"What should I do?"

"Go get the rest of it out."

"I don't have the urge anymore. I think it went back up."

4

Frankie rigged up the vacuum and handed it to me. I'd make it about an inch before it inhaled a branch or a frog and jammed the thing like a throat with a fish bone caught in it. Then we'd have to shut the machine off, pull the vacuum out of the pool, smash it against something until the passage unclogged, and restart it. Not that it even made much of a difference. The water looked and smelled like the lower Ganges. Thick enough with sludge for birds to tiptoe across the slimy film.

Ralph woke up and began calling the filter box every racial epitaph in the book, and some new gems I'd never heard before too. Then he stood up, dropped the hammer he was using toward his feet, and football punted it across the yard.

"Too bad he didn't kick that hammer right into his face," Frankie said.

Ralph walked over and took the vacuum pole from

my hands. "Let me vacuum for a while. If I don't take a break, I'm going to shoot that filter."

"What should I do?" I asked Frankie.

"Go check the filter baskets. Last time I was here we found a dead kitten in one."

These mystery holes I had to open were my least favorite part of the job. I thought back to the first pool and remembered the way the snake's skin had felt.

I knelt down, stuck my finger through the hole, and popped the lid off. Then I held it up to shield my face.

Nothing flew out.

I hunched over the filter basket and saw a dead animal being devoured by dung flies. Hair swam off the body, leaving a mass of pink pulp. It looked like a naked baby bobbing gently in the pool's current.

Judging by the size, I guessed a raccoon.

"Hey guys," I called. "Come look at this."

Frankie picked up his safety pole and held it like a tomahawk. "Is it alive?"

I shook my head.

Frankie and Ralph came over to the hole and looked down.

"Whoa," Ralph said. "That's huge."

We walked to the other filter basket and opened it. Something almost as big was dead in that one as well, and it had a long rat tail.

Ralph looked at us and smiled for the first time. "Go get the nets," he said. "Let's play a game."

The others may have had their doubts, but Ralph definitely got *it*. The kind of guy who'd say, "A good hamburger should be flipped only once." A legend of many horseshoe tournaments. I imagined that whatever game he fished out of his beer brain would probably be a good one.

5

We stood with two pool skimmers, a dead animal in each net, stationed at the far side of the pool. Frankie had the raccoon fetus in his net. I had the potential opossum corpse in mine.

Ralph had gone to his police car and come back with a Glock .22. He positioned his arm in an L shape, with the gun pointed up into the air.

"The game is called Catapult," he said. "When I fire, launch your animal over the house as hard as you can. Whoever's lands furthest gets the last beer."

He fired the gun. It shook every window on the block. Frankie and I swung our arms like we were firing bombs over a wall. Then we all ran to the front yard.

The raccoon's body was lying in the street, just passed the mailbox. Little puddles of flesh and slime were left where the body had bounced.

"Congratulations, Frankie," Ralph said. "I'm gonna call you 'Muscles Marinara' from now on."

He gave Frankie the last beer. Frankie started to open it, but then he handed it to me and said, "It's blood beer. I don't want it."

But where was the opossum? There were no bushes in the front yard to hide a creature. No vultures flew overhead. Everything was right in place.

"I knew this was a terrible idea," Frankie said. "God is going to punish us because we played with the dead."

"Frankie, come on," I laughed. "This is not divine intervention."

"How would you know?"

"Because ... if God was paying attention, he would've been punishing us long before this."

But when I thought about it, I realized that the Universe *did* seem to have a personal vendetta against us and our line of work. Maybe we were being cursed by the Almighty after all.

Ralph scratched the gun against his head and did a pivot. I chugged the beer while studying the street. There was a feeling of strange nostalgia. It was all so familiar. I knew these houses. I'd been here before.

"Oh no," Ralph said, pointing up.

The opossum body was tangled in the cable wires that connected to the roof of the house. A 3lb. blob of dead flesh, dripping brown pool scum.

"Way to go," Ralph said. "Let's get this pool finished before that old guy tries to turn on Jeopardy."

6

Ralph picked up the hammer he had kicked and went back to fight the filter box. From the sounds coming from behind the bushes, I was certain he was still losing.

I pretended to vacuum while Frankie screwed all the grommets back into the concrete. I was pretty sure air bubbles were popping around the pool. They kept happening in my periphery so I wasn't positive.

"Frankie," I said, "if this water is fresh enough to grow trees, don't you think ... other things might be in here?"

"Like what?"

"Three headed snakes. The Loch Ness Monster."

"Shit. I didn't even think about that. I was just about to stick my arm in."

Frankie had to unscrew the plugs that get twisted into the return holes when a pool is closed for the season. These plugs secured the lines so no winter water would freeze in them and crack the pipes. And they were all about a foot under the surface.

"Go ask Ralph for his gun," I said. "I'll shoot anything that moves."

Frankie went over to Ralph. I heard him say, "Oh yeah, it's a dangerous job." Ralph nodded his head and stood up. He checked the safety on his gun, then underhanded it over the bushes to Frankie. "Watch your face," he told him. "She's got a kick."

Frankie passed me the gun, butt first, and said, "Make sure you hit anything you shoot at. Otherwise, we'll have to replace the liner." Then he squatted down and stuck his hands in the pool.

I kept a lookout on top of the waterfall.

"At least it's a hundred degrees out," I said. "Anything reptilian should be too lazy to hunt us."

Thick black smoke began billowing up from behind the shrubs where Ralph was working. Little fireworks spiraled off into the air and fizzled out. Then rumblings started like a revving motorcycle engine.

"Everything okay, Ralph?" I asked.

The filter box torched up like an IED. Ralph flew back about ten feet with flames sprouting from his head.

"Frankie," I said, "Ralph's on fire!" Then I tossed the gun into a bush and started shouting, "HELP!"

Ralph was rolling around the grass, digging his palms into his eyes. Frankie scooped up a handful of dirt on his way over and threw it onto Ralph's smoldering head.

"I'm blind!" Ralph cried. "Blinded by electricity."

I grabbed a hose and dragged it to them. Ralph took his hands off his eyes. They were bulging in a terrible way. Black ash colored his face like he'd failed out of a minstrel show.

"Ralph, we've got to get you to a hospital," Frankie

said.

"There's no time, Frankie. This pool has to be fin-ished today."

Frankie and I each took one of his arms and lifted him up.

"Should we call you an ambulance?" I asked.

Ralph filled up his hands with hose water and tried to scrub out his eyes. "No. I'll drive myself. I called out sick today. If an ambulance comes they'll find out I've been here cleaning pools, and the captain will really have my ass."

Frankie made a peace-sign and put it up to Ralph's face. "Can you even see? How many fingers am I hold-ing up?"

"I've got the squad car. I'll put the siren on full blast. Everyone has to get out of the way." He got up and did a half-hearted salute, like a commander who had come up short for his troops. Then he walked away with his head down, leaving the privates to clean up his mess.

We stood there in a kind of battlefield shock until we heard his police siren fading down the block. Then Frankie said, "Thank God that fist-pumping jerk-off is gone. He couldn't plan a two-car funeral without fucking it up."

But Ralph did leave behind a small bit of wisdom, at least for me. I thought about the Queen. I thought about how eventually the jig is up, and the card game of wom-en comes to a close. And when the dust clears, if you don't pick the right one, you are cursed to walk the earth like a slobbering buffalo. A crude and ugly animal that nobody wants - your deformation out there for all to see. Through natural selection and biology, you can be a fail-ure on every level, and the earth will be no better a place for keeping you around.

I had just seen my future. Being in Ralph's presence was like staring into a deranged crystal ball. I understood, finally, what it meant to lose for good.

I'll quit drinking, I thought. And cut my hair. Take it *all* more seriously.

I went back to the waterfall and saw Ralph's gun lying right where I had dropped it. I picked it up. I put my finger behind the trigger and spun the gun once over my knuckles, Jesse James style.

I could kill anything I wanted.

The realization put a big smile on my face.

I buried the gun at the bottom of the toolbox and didn't mention it to Frankie.

7

The old man came back outside right after Ralph left. A concerned neighbor had called to see if a meth lab had just erupted next door.

"Everything is fine," Frankie lied. "Sometimes you cross two wires the wrong way. Hazard of the trade."

The old man nodded like he understood, but could anyone really understand a backyard pool? A big hole in the ground filled with water. Surrounded by plastic. An Erector Set of underground pipes connected to a computer in a box. Wires came out of the earth and disappeared back in. Some levers and gadgets were pulled and punched. Sometimes it all worked. Sometimes everything exploded. Somehow this made sense. And no one ever stopped to ask how it had all come to be this way.

Frankie called the Boss and explained the last hour. Our directions were to get everything in order but the filter box. The Boss said he'd swing by in a few days and take care of it.

We were also instructed to meet him for lunch so he could get more weed from Frankie.

"No way," I said. "That's our weed."

"It's *my* weed. He'll buy us lunch and drinks."

"I'll be abstaining from alcohol from this moment forward. To invest in my future."

"No more drinking?"

"Not until I own a house."

"We'll see."

8

The only thing left to do was screw the last grommet back in under the waterfall. I pointed at the mound of concrete. "Why would anyone install something this ridiculous?"

"The waterfall ties the backyard together."

"No, it doesn't. It looks like someone fucked up a block of concrete and stuck it at the edge of the pool."

"Concrete is the most beautiful thing man has ever created. It is our crowning achievement as a species. When you become a master pool boy you'll understand these things."

The old man came back out with a cat on a leash and a cup of tea. He had a VFW trucker hat on now. Loose rolls of skin were coming untucked and flopping out from under the sides.

There were two lawn chairs at the shallow end of the pool. He held the cat and put the teacup on one. Then he sat down with the cat on his lap. He scratched the cat's chin. Scratched its ears. The cat never stopped frowning.

"What do they think we are?" Frankie asked. "Live entertainment?"

"I hate it when cats stare at me."

Frankie looked at the waterfall, then the pool cover we'd folded on the lawn. "Before we get to the waterfall let's put the cover back in the bag."

"Should I get the power washer?"

"Don't bother. It's going to look like shit no matter what."

"Let's just throw it out then."

"He's going to have a fit if we leave him without a pool cover *and* an exploded filter."

"But if we save it he's going to make us glue it back together when we close the pool."

"Yeah, I know," he groaned. "And he'll be sitting there with that ugly cat staring at us the whole time."

I went to a shed at the back corner of the yard and found the cover bag. Small holes had been chewed through most of it and it smelled terrible. I tucked my shirt over my nose and brought the bag back to Frankie.

He propped it open and we tried to lift the cover from the grass. All the crud that had caked onto it oozed like slug guts. It was like trying to pull a wet fish off the ground.

Frankie kicked me out of the way and lifted the cover himself. I got on my knees and held the bag open as he powerbombed it down from over his head.

"Who's better than me?" he asked.

"Nobody?"

"Noooo-body."

The old man took the cat's paws and clapped them together. Then, in a cat voice, he said, "Mr. Muffins is so impressed with the pool boys."

We pretended we didn't hear him.

"All right, bro," Frankie said, "now the hard part." He pointed at the grommet under the waterfall. "We can't leave until that gets screwed in."

It was impossible from any angle. We tried to reach the grommet from both sides of the waterfall, but it had been installed dead in the middle. Without standing in the pool there was only one way to get to it.

"You're going to hold my legs," Frankie instructed, "and I'm going to hang over the top of the waterfall and screw it in."

He duct taped an extended Allen key to the end of one of the safety poles. The grommets had a hexagon shaped hole in their heads. A clockwise turn with the Allen key would send it spiraling back into the concrete.

"Can't the Boss just do this?" I asked.

"We're being paid to open this pool *the right way*. You think the Boss is better than me?"

"No."

"Who's better than me?"

I didn't answer. Frankie got onto the waterfall and laid face down on the extended piece of slate. He crawled to the edge and was about to go over headfirst. I was going to hold his ankles as he hung completely vertical over the pool.

He rolled over and pointed the safety pole at me. "If you drop me you'll be joining Ralph in the emergency room."

I stood on the soles of his flip flops. Then I bent down, putting all my strength into a grapple around his ankles.

He climbed over and was hanging upside down, his head about three inches above the water line.

"How's it going?" I asked.

"I can't get the damn key into the grommet."

He sucked in a deep angry breath. I could feel the veins in his legs hardening.

A big splash came from the middle of the pool.

"Did you see that?" Frankie asked.

I slid my hand up his thigh to peer over the edge.

"Bro don't drop me," he said. "I don't know what's going on in this pool."

An air bubble burst close to his dangling head.

"Get me out of here!" he ordered. "It's coming for me!"

I tried to pull him up but he was flailing too hard. I kept one hand on his ankle and clutched his bathing suit with the other.

The whole waterfall started to shake.

Frankie attempted an inverted swing up, but it was too much stress on the piece of slate I was on. His bathing suit came loose, and as I scrambled to grab him, the slate broke off.

"Kowabunga!" he said.

We both went headfirst into the muddy water. The tree limbs felt like eels wrapping themselves around my body. I opened my eyes to look for Frankie and got bombarded by little two-armed larvae. I could feel them digging behind my retinas, heading straight for my brain.

Suddenly, a hand clamped down on my hair and pulled me out of the pool. I landed on the concrete, sat up, and blew a huge snot rocket out of each nostril. Then Frankie stuck a cigarette into my mouth and said, "We're going to smell like swamphole for a month."

The old man was laughing and slapping his knee like he'd never seen anything so funny. Even the cat looked like it was smiling.

What kind of a world was this? My ancestors got on a boat. They left the Italian coast for the gold-paved roads of America. And the bloodlines landed me here, at a death pool that probably had piranhas swimming in it.

And I had to clean it for $10 an hour.

"Forget the grommet," Frankie said. "I'm going to fill up a garbage can so we can take a bath."

9

Frankie dragged one of the garbage cans from our truck into the backyard. He put the hose in it and dropped three pucks of chlorine in as it was filling up with water.

"We look like refugees," I said. "If the neighbors see us they're going to think this guy adopted us out of a floating bathtub."

Smoke started rising from the garbage can. Frankie used the hose to stir the water like it was a big pot of soup.

"Okay," he said. "Hop in."

"This stuff is banned as a weapon and white phosphorus isn't? Are you sure this is safe?"

"I do it all the time. It's way better than a shower."

I climbed in. The water burned every pore in my skin. I rubbed quickly and felt myself drying out. Then I traded places with Frankie. All the moisture in my body evaporated like I had been covered in the soot of Pompeii.

"Frankie, if I don't have water right now I'm going to die. I think I'm disintegrating."

He shot me in the face with the hose. "Rub-a-dub-dub, bro."

10

We walked to the front yard stiff as stick figures - all of our joints chalk-white and dehydrated from the chlorine.

I looked at the neighborhood again, trying to place

it. "Frankie, why does this look so familiar?"

"Remember our one semester of community college? We used to drive through here on the way to Brookdale."

I finally recognized the road. I hadn't seen it since winters earlier, when the snows melted and turned the small creeks into big angry rivers. The turmoil of the water, loud and gray, right before the spring came and the stems of purple crocuses began to break through the morning frost.

I memorized the thaw at the end of silent winter each week on my way to class, just a few miles away.

I was thinking about riding a bike to California in those days, too.

I thought, for the first time ever, that my parents knew more than I gave them credit for.

It was 1:10 p.m.

CHAPTER ELEVEN

1

"Where are we meeting the Boss?" I asked.

"The Shooter Shack. Happy hour started at one. I see lots of tequila shots in our future."

The only real benefit of working manual labor is that when you cut it straight down the line, your co-workers are all alcoholics.

We parked near a bulkhead where the pavement met the bay. The low tide stench of clams hung over the street. Seagulls circled above a docking crab boat.

I pointed to a little gazebo overlooking the water. "That's where I kissed Queen Jac two nights ago."

Frankie pinched his nose and said, "I hope it smelled better than it does now."

We walked into The Shooter Shack and sat down at the bar with the Boss. He was already halfway through a pitcher of beer. Three tequila shots with limes were neatly lined up.

"Maybe I'll have just one," I said to Frankie. "No reason to be rude."

"That didn't take long."

I held up my shot. "Lord," I proclaimed like a prophet, "thank you for giving me the strength to beat my own limitations."

The three of us put our glasses together.

"Salud," Frankie said.

We took the shots and sucked on the limes.

"Order some lunch, boys," the Boss told us. "The sliders are only $2."

"Twelve sliders, sir," I said to the bartender. "And a pot of coffee."

"Do you want cream and sugar?" he asked.

"No. Just give me the pot. And stick a straw in it if you don't mind."

The Boss asked Frankie about Ralph: "I know what he's going to say. It's always, 'It's not my fault' or 'I didn't pass out on her patio because I was drunk, it was heat exhaustion'." He punched his fist into his palm and dug it in. "This is all my in-laws' fault. How can two people produce so many idiots? What should I do, Frankie?"

Frankie had been an employee of American Pools for seven years. He was just about family by now. If he wanted to throw Ralph under the bus it was his call. But there is a tenet in America, one that might supersede all the others: Don't fuck with another man's money. No one took the rules more seriously than Frankie, so I figured he'd cover for Ralph. Either way though, it involved family. It was no business of mine to be hearing any of this.

I excused myself and went to the bathroom. The bar had been a honky tonk until the last hurricane hit. Everything was destroyed except two saloon doors that hung loosely in front of the bathroom. They were a sort of Bayshore mascot now. Everyone who didn't go to college got them tattooed on their bodies like a shitty gang brand.

I pushed the doors open and went inside. A big worm wearing a cowboy hat was painted on the wall directly in front of me. It had one eye closed, winking at me. I spit into my piss stream, then turned around to wash my hands. On my way out I looked at the worm again. It made eye contact no matter where I was standing.

Frankie and the Boss went out to the truck to split up the weed. I took another shot and saw a pool table by the far wall. It slumped a bit to one side. Somehow in all my nights getting drunk at The Shack I'd never noticed it before.

"Can I get a game?" I asked the bartender.

"It's $1 per round. And I need an ID."

I gave him my license then pointed to the Boss' half-drunk pitcher. "Put it on his tab."

He swung two pool cues over the bar and handed me a token for the table. "You look like a good American so I want to let you know - a man named Javier is going to show up soon and tell you that's *his* table."

"Who's Javier?"

"Javier calls himself El Diablo de Español, but he's really some immigrant cocksucker who thinks we're only in Iraq for oil. I used to kick people like that out. Now we get sued for it."

"What happened to patriotism?"

"This Javier handles a pool cue like it's his third arm so don't let him hustle you."

"I think I can take him. Maybe I'll win one for the home team."

He gave me a smirk and started wiping off the bar. "We need a win. The whole country's going to hell in a hand basket."

The pool table ate my first token and when I got the second the bartender told me to use my heel and give the side a good horse kick as the token rolled in. I did and the table sounded like it broke in half, but the balls spilled out into the slot in one big pile. I felt connected to it. I liked the oak legs marred like an old tree. I liked the felt on the bed that had given up its green long ago, weathered almost raw by dirty hands and sloppy shots.

It was the kind of table a real man could make some money on.

I needed to learn the angles. I knew Javier was familiar with the soul of the table and I didn't want to just give him layup after layup. I dropped the cue ball and it rolled a little to the left. I picked it up and dropped it at the other end. Same thing.

I could feel the bartender behind me, observing my preparation. A motorcycle roared outside. I chalked up my stick and watched the front door. Ready for whatever was coming in.

The door opened like an old western. A cloud of dust surrounded a man twirling a toothpick between his fingers. A leather jacket fit tight around his chest. Boots dented the wooden floor under his step. It was like watching John Dillinger size up a bank.

He smiled at the bartender and the bartender pointed at me.

Javier had a stride like he'd just jumped off a horse. He pushed his hair back and put the toothpick in his mouth. It seemed like a moment he'd been preparing for his whole life, some sort of showdown.

I looked out the window and saw the shadows of trees starting to pull east. It wasn't high noon, but it was close enough.

I grabbed the triangle rack off the wall and spun it

like a basketball between my palms. Then I put it on the table and folded my arms.

Javier gave me the slow nod of a cowboy. He spread his arms and his jacket slid down his back. He took it off and hung it around a chair and said, "You're on my table."

"The dollar I just paid says it's my table."

"Then it looks like we're playing for keeps. Rack em' up, kid."

I put each ball into the triangle, alternating stripes and solids all the way around. Then I rolled the triangle forward and draped the last knuckle of each finger over the wood, securing the balls together.

"You should break," I said. "Gentleman's game."

Javier opened a clip and pulled out two $5 bills. He slapped them on the oak rim of the table and said, "Go to Manhattan if you want a gentleman."

Frankie and the Boss came back into the bar.

"Frankie," I called. "Get the $16 the Boss owes me. We've got a game going."

"You've cost me $30 since you've been here," the Boss said. "Fuck you."

They walked over and stood behind me. Frankie leaned in and said, "Do you even play pool?"

"I spent a lot of time in college avoiding class. What do you think?"

"Can we hurry this up?" Javier interrupted. "Real Madrid is playing Barcelona in an hour."

The Boss took out his wallet and threw $10 down.

"Now back up," I said to him. "Let me breathe."

I broke on a slight angle to the right. The slump of the table allowed additional roll after all the balls ricocheted off the wall. Two solids dropped in.

"You know what, Javier?" I said. "Since *I'm* a gentleman, I'll take stripes."

The break was decent, but not great. A big clump of balls hung out in the middle. In case I missed I didn't want to give Javier a clear table, so I started chipping balls off the edges.

I sunk two stripes and then I scratched.

Javier set his stick down and did a jump back like a matador. He was good. He didn't just have game; he knew how to give a show. Before each shot he called the pocket. That became too easy for him. He started acing combo shots. One of my stripes was in the way. He banked his balls, hit mine, and the stripe and solids rolled together toward the hole. His fell in and mine stopped. It hovered right around the pocket, then rolled away.

All the hope I'd had for winning his $10 was quickly disappearing. The drink with the Queen. The single rose I could buy her.

He didn't just beat me; he turned my pool game into amateur hour. The Boss didn't even stay for the end. The table told the story. All but two stripes sat like tombstones. My stick never touched the chalk after my break run.

Javier held his pool cue like a guitar and pretended to pluck individual strings. Then he started strumming wildly like a mariachi on fire. "You came to the church of the good hustler," he said. "Check in any time you like. But you can never leave."

"Enough with the Nietzsche crap," Frankie said to him. "Go flamenco your ass to a rodeo and get fucked by a bull."

2

Javier came outside and put a cigarette in his mouth. He

gestured his head, saying, "Hey loser, light me up."

I pulled a lighter from my pocket and handed it to him.

"You know why you're not a man?" he asked.

I knew. I had this body, getting fatter and hairier every day, but nothing inside had changed. Nobody ever told me I'd grow into this - the shell of a man with nothing figured out.

"No," I said.

He pointed at his motorcycle. "You don't have one of those."

"Why are you still here?"

"Where would I go?"

"I thought my friend told you to go get fucked by a bull?"

3

I went back inside. The sun followed me through the door and lit up the bottles behind the bar like little diamonds were floating inside of them. It gave me that feeling a kid gets staring at rainbow colored candy. Booze is like candy for adults, I realized. It's our reward for getting through things that suck.

I walked to the news rack and looked at three piles of curated garbage: disappointing local news, horrible country news, and total dystopian world news.

I picked up the local.

ASBURY PARK PRESS

Buffet-Style Restaurants Warned of Terror Threat

The State Department of Health has asked municipal health departments to contact restaurants with salad bars and buffets to inform them of a potential terrorist threat involving poisoned food.

The threat, which was reported by CBS News on Monday and deemed "credible" by the Department of Homeland Security, involved terrorists poisoning salad bars and buffets with cyanide and ricin.

Salad bars and buffets need to be closely monitored by restaurant staff and any suspicious activity must be reported immediately.

Attached to the front page of the same paper was an old message from New Jersey's favorite son: Chris Christie. Another Governor riding a shit-train through the middle-class he had sworn to protect. His throat hung over his collar like an overfed pug; a perfect receptacle for the cocks of the 1% to ejaculate down while he threw up rules and regulations invented to decimate anyone whose life relied on a hard-earned pension.

The note was a reprint from barely a year earlier. An ugly reminder of what he'd said as candidate Christie, and the reality of what he'd done since becoming Governor.

(the note: written by Chris Christie)

An Open Letter To The Teachers Of New Jersey

Lately, there has been some misinformation circulated falsely, by supporters of Governor Corzine, suggesting I would attempt to diminish or take away teachers' pensions and benefits. Let me be clear - nothing could be further from the truth. The claim that any harm would come to your pension should I be elected Governor is absolutely untrue. It is a 100% lie. Your pension will be protected when I am elected

Governor. We may disagree on some issues, but I know we agree on what's most important – delivering the best education we can for our kids.

The note went on of course, as bullshit often does. It trickles out of a few open mouths like the first puddles forming around a clogged sewer. And before anyone knows it the town's flooded with the stuff. People are swimming in it. Dogs are lapping it up until their tongues turn green with sores. Suddenly everyone's drowning in an endless sea of total shit. And upon each stroke back toward sanity, the shoreline, once so familiar and tangible, floats off like a mirage in an abstract and soulless desert.

Good American citizens woke up one morning last November. They read that note from Chris Christie and felt safe. They watched their children catch one more dream in the deep pocket of early morning sleep. Then, with that last image of innocence in their guiding hands, they lined up to vote.

And once again a fat reptile emerged straight from the Republican lizard tank; a shape shifter anxious for destruction, blowing fire out of his anus and swinging the hatchet down on the middle-class he had just sworn to protect.

Christie barely got a night's sleep before attacking the teachers' pensions. But it didn't matter; his letter had already pushed him across the finish line. And no American who works for a living has time to sort the half-truths from the lies.

I thought of the pained faces on everyone who had reread Christie's words this morning. Wondering why they were subscribing to this drivel. Shaking their heads. Drinking another cup of coffee. But this time deeper.

Blacker.

New Jersey never played by the same rules as the rest of the land, but this time they hadn't even bothered with secrecy. Christie immediately cut $1 billion in aid from the schools, and when a teacher asked him why, he said, "I'm tired of you people."

The reign of our 55th Governor stunk like a fart cloud that never dissipated. And he was the kind of megalomaniac that didn't want to just be hailed as a martyr; he wanted to be thanked for it. "The schools are failure factories," he'd said right after the election. "Put the money where families have hope."

While the youth saw a motivated hemorrhoid, the Republican Party drooled over their new fiscal conservative. They finally had a lapdog brave enough to stand up to a strong union in an organized state.

Christie sat in hot tubs with the King of Jordan. He shared lap dances with Donald Trump down in Atlantic City. And when it came time to balance the budget, he said it was the teachers who were leeching off the taxpayers of New Jersey.

The middle-class practically killed each other overnight. And in a state where most can hardly afford to eat, the idiots knelt down and chanted, "Yes, Mr. Rich Man, anything you say."

After all, it had to be somebody's fault the Garden State was in a total free-fall. The billionaires live behind gates. It's easier to blame the neighbor you can *see* with summers off. And a convenient blame will always find open arms. It sleeps in the Walmart parking lot. It fits right in between the barbecue and "the game."

4

"Those headlines are enough to make a man jump in the ocean and swim for Portugal," I said.

"That's why I don't read the news," the Boss said. "I hate the government. But I support the troops."

Surfers came into the bar and ordered Jager shots. The Boss threw $20 on the counter and paid for everyone to have a vial of the black brew. I hated Jager, but everything goes down smooth when you're on the ass-end of a sixteen-hour workday.

"Of all life's choices," I said to the Boss, "why would you start a pool company?"

"It's six months of work every year. I've got a brother with two degrees who has to work every Saturday."

"Imagine being the first asshole who decided they were going to get up and go to work? Why didn't everyone else in the village kick the shit out of them?"

"Let me tell you something my grandfather once told me: 'You're not supposed to like your job. That's why it's called work'. No one's gonna pay you to be happy. This ain't Sweden ... thank God."

We drank a lot more. Frankie and the Boss went out to smoke. I ate my sliders and watched lazy waves lap onto brown sand through the bar window.

If this was the rest of my life the epitaph would be brief: *Get Out While You're Young.*

Where do the other kinds go? The ones who keep all night roadhouses in business. The people who say, "fuck it" and walk away. Aren't we all born to be out there? Servants to nothing but our stomachs and hearts. Never saying "yes sir" to anyone who doesn't deserve it.

But freedom doesn't seem like such a priority these days. Even the rock stars are friends with bankers. And if you are unlucky enough to be born with the gypsy blood, you'll survive in the modern world about as well as a freed test monkey who suddenly has to pay rent.

Somehow, while being as good as everyone else at a day job, the artist also has to be the best at night, when the typewriter keys can flash and bang like machine gun rounds out of the deep trench. Watching words hammer onto the page from the firing squad of your mind. Where the fear can be faced. Where you can enter and exit the same night a different man.

You think like that when you're young.

But the years move faster than the typewriter keys. Eventually we're all forced onto our hands and knees for a job. And it owns you long before you start getting paid. The hours burn while you sum up your own worth on a piece of paper. The hopeless weeks of sitting around, hoping some middle-manager finds your resume and decides it's worthy. They demand a cup of your DNA. They demand your gas tank. And by the time they hire you, the trauma is so fresh, you're just thankful for a desk near a window.

And that's fine, I guess.

It's been worse.

But how had the scales tipped so far so fast? Somewhere on this quest for the dirty dollar we accidentally imprisoned ourselves. The point of no return vanished long ago. And as the bow of time drifts forward, all the dreams from childhood boil away for the only two true victories that can put some dignity back into a worker's soul - getting paid what you're worth and killing your boss.

I watched the Boss through the bar window. Vulnerable. Exposed. I can do one of those right now, I thought. I can kill him and be free.

But then what? Even if I found the Ace of Pentacles on his corpse, and a bag of money fell out of the sky, what exactly would I do with it? I'd probably just spend my days lying on the beach. A beach I could walk to any time. A beach I could see right now. But something was always going to hold me back.

I saw a future with seashells in a jar and a painting of a white sand beach.

My dream was going to end up as a painting on my bathroom wall.

I knew it more than I'd ever known anything. I was going to have a beach themed bathroom.

I was going to be like everyone else.

CHAPTER TWELVE

1

My phone lit up as I was dozing off on our way to the next pool. It was a text from Queen Jac: *Let's paint this whole town yellow.*

"Frankie," I said. "I love her."

"What are you going to say back?"

"Nothing. I just hit Cee-lo. I rolled a 4-5-6. The only thing I can do from here is ruin it."

Frankie pulled into a Wawa. We had been smoking about ten cigarettes an hour since dawn. I swore each one I lit would be my last, but that was impossible. We seemed to be smoking more with each miserable hour, and we needed another pack.

I waited in the truck while he went to buy cigarettes. A long, green praying mantis climbed in my window and looked at me. Her eyes seemed to be contemplating an afterlife other creatures never considered. Who was she praying to?

"Who is your God?" I asked.

I stuck my hand out for her and she walked on. Her little eyes locked on mine like she was trying to figure out my purpose. Or maybe she was trying to tell me something.

"Are you here to give me information?" I laughed. "What is it? Are sasquatches real?"

No reaction.

"Was 9/11 an inside job?"

Nothing.

"Are you hungry?"

Her green mantis head went down and up. Like a nod.

I mouthed a slow motion, "Whoa." I could see that she was waiting for me to do something. When I didn't move, she dipped her head again.

"We're ... communicating."

Was this a superpower?

Why was I chosen?

Did I have an arch nemesis?

She lifted one of her legs and kicked herself in the head. Somehow I knew this gesture meant she wanted to kick me in the head. Probably for being very dumb.

"All right, fine. Let's get you fed."

I looked in our old water bottles and found two drowned bugs. "We've got appetizers!"

The mantis clutched onto my hand and I walked her to a bush. I turned the water bottles over and drained the dead bugs out onto the curb, right in her view.

"Goodbye, friend." I ran my finger gently over her head. "I wish we'd had more time together."

I gave a thumbs up to the sky for bugs. For the Queen. For best friends. Then I walked to a liquor store across the street and stole a flask bottle of Jack Daniel's.

A bum kid with neck acne was sitting on a milk crate behind the counter. His head was slumped over in his lap. He didn't wake up when I walked into the store. He didn't wake up as I reached behind the counter and grabbed the bottle of Jack. I would've taken the register too, but the kid seemed in as bad a shape as I was.

There's no reason to crowd tomorrow's unemployment line, I thought.

2

I climbed back into the truck and spun the radio dial to Q104.3. "No Surrender" came on. I reached to change the station, but I couldn't bring myself to do it.

"Now on the street tonight the lights grow dim
The walls of my room are closing in
There's a war outside still raging
You say it ain't ours anymore to win"

It was the first time I understood the lyrics.

I knew then that my youth was gone.

Bruce just couldn't be enjoyed unless you were a man on the grind.

A pretty blonde in a Monmouth University shirt walked down the sidewalk with her dog. It was a little white terrier with two pink bows in its hair. Frankie came out of Wawa with a cigarette already lit. He looked the girl up and down and made a face of approval.

The dog was trying to get some attention. It kept barking at the girl but she was busy texting. Finally the dog stopped, retched from almost its tail to its mouth, and threw up all over the girl's feet.

She screamed and jumped around while the dog wagged at her with no remorse.

I couldn't have said it any better, I thought.

CHAPTER THIRTEEN

The Hole In The Liner

1

"I'm too drunk to do any more work," I said.

I handed Frankie the Jack Daniel's bottle.

"I'm driving, bro."

Can't quit now, I thought. I drank most of the bottle and dropped it onto the floor. It banged and clanged against the metal bolts below my seat every time we hit a pothole.

On the back of a receipt, I wrote:

To the Queen,

It came to me just now. For days I've heard nothing but your voice. I'm a mess, and all I can hear is you saying, "It's about time." I've offended everyone I've seen since you. I want to hear your voice, not theirs, so I don't listen. I want to see your face, not theirs, so I don't look. Like the ancients before us, let's drink the wine, smoke the stash, paint the caves. Like the ancients before us, let's dance, let's conquer, let's disappear.

I won't sign this. Nothing this good should end.

I crumbled up the receipt and threw it out the window. If she knew I was falling for her the mystery would be gone, and right now it was about all I had going for me.

"Two years ago," I said. "That was it. We were going to move to Los Angeles and surf. Why didn't we?"

"I love Jersey. Anything you could want is right here. We've got the beach. The people make sense. You can't get food like this anywhere else."

He had a point, but was pizza enough to kiss our dreams goodbye? We were suddenly older than I ever thought we'd be. There was nothing cute about running to LA anymore.

Frankie pulled the truck to the side of the road. There was a lot about forty feet wide. A crumbled foundation was still sort of visible. A few plants had started to spring up.

"Look," he said.

"Where?"

"Right there."

"I don't see anything."

"You don't see *anything*? Come on, let's take a hike."

He got out of the truck. I looked at the vacant lot. Another massacred piece of nature. There'll be a Wawa here next time I drive by, I thought.

"I'm good," I said. "Let's just go."

"No way, bro. We're in God's country."

"I'll take a picture."

"Smell the air. Look at the grass. You need to appreciate these things."

"Appreciate what? A dog wouldn't piss here."

"A Jersey dog would. Someone who understood his

home would piss here. You think you're too good for all this? You think you deserve better? What do you do? All you do is complain."

"Yeah, you're right. Boy, that grass is just beautiful. Wow. Those two houses right next to us really Feng Shui the lot."

"Always with the sarcasm. At least I have pride. I'm a Jersey boy and I know it."

"Well, I have nothing. And I hate this shit."

Frankie gave up. He marched back to the truck. I put my head against the dashboard to emphasize my unwillingness to enjoy life.

"Can't you just get published?" he asked.

"It's not as easy as it sounds. My story has been rejected by everyone on the internet."

"What's it about?"

They always asked this question.

I hated this question.

"Remember when we were little and we thought the news was there to help us?"

"I don't watch the news. That's why I'm such a happy person." He smiled to himself like he'd just had a breakthrough.

"Anyway," I said, "there was this story that said half of your pillow's weight is microscopic bugs living on the pillowcase. But whether I changed the case every couple of days or once a year, I never felt any difference."

"I don't get it. Is that a story?"

"Yeah."

"What did you call it?"

"*The Pillowcase.*"

"Jesus, that's terrible. I would've rejected you, too."

2

I kept nodding off due to the drink and the heat. But there was no way to stay asleep - it felt like a beatnik caravan was winding through my head.

I read the Queen's text again and thought about a field of sunflowers, and her naked body dancing with their green stems and golden faces under a China-plate sky.

It calmed my nerves.

I fell into a dream. I couldn't hear anything but I could see a man conducting a piece of music. Two notes danced together on a page with the wands of his fingers. He was working in an empty symphony hall, and each time the notes touched staffs, fireflies filled the room.

The bugs flew out an open door and I saw the Queen and me driving down the Jersey Turnpike. The conductor's song was playing on my car's radio. I could finally hear it: a verse of falling rain. A chorus of kissing rabbits. The most beautiful song ever written. The Queen unbuckled her seatbelt and leaned over with a sinning grin. And right as I closed my eyes, she grabbed my neck and whispered, "Drive this motherfucker like you stole it."

I woke up and slapped myself in the face. "Frankie, pull over. I've got to piss like a pregnant lady."

"Hang on."

He stuck his arm out the window as a stop signal. Then he cut the truck across the highway into a McDonald's.

I grabbed a packet of barbecue sauce on the way to the bathroom and licked it clean. The dry rot taste of whiskey had left a nasty phlegm caked onto my tongue.

Frankie and I stood side by side at the urinals. He was pushed right up against the porcelain but it didn't sound like anything was coming out.

"Frankie, have you pissed yet?"

"No."

"Have you gone at all since the piranha pool?"

"No, bro. I think I broke something."

We walked back to the truck in silence. It was pool season. He'd have to wait until at least October to see a doctor.

3

"What's next?" I asked.

"The stripper's house."

"Frankie, the Universe *is* smiling at us. If anything can fix your dick this is probably it."

"It's a guy stripper. His name is The Hammer."

"All of the stripper pools in all of the world and we had to walk into a dudes? This was our chance."

"What chance?"

"To be real pool boys, you know? Get laid on the job while the husband is at work."

"That never happens."

"Never?"

"Bro, how could that happen? You're either opening pools, which means you fall in and smell like total shit. Or you're cleaning pools, so you're covered with chemicals and dead animals. Then you close the pool. And just as you're almost done, when you're finally pulling the cover back out of the bag, it drenches you in mouse piss. If somebody *wanted* to sleep with me I'd run. I had Chlamydia once. I'm not trying to go home with the plague."

4

There was genius in that stripper's head. A man whose father had probably said, "Just do it," and he listened. The rest of the country was out there losing, but The Hammer figured out how to skip student loans and make a fortune taking off his pants.

Two Maseratis were lounging in The Hammer's driveway like lions in a food coma - full of gas and stressed about nothing. Certainly not for the zip code in Monmouth County they were sleeping in; where foreclosure signs outnumbered trees and property taxes rose like debt ceilings.

"What's the issue at this house?" I asked.

"Just a hole in the liner. We'll be in and out."

I might've been fooled at the first stop, but by now I knew there was no such thing as "in and out" in pool time. It was inevitable that something would go wrong. And we would be left to find a solution that hopefully held until the following week, when the next crew of pool boys would be blamed for our mistakes.

"I'll bet you $20 we're here for at least an hour," I said.

"You don't have any money."

"But I can't lose."

"You always lose. And now you've jinxed us."

I could hear ambient noise coming from Monmouth Park Racetrack. Somewhere, on the other side of this suburban ocean of mailboxes and vinyl, a race was beginning.

I pictured the line of beautiful horses waiting for the gunfire. Families with coolers sitting in boisterous anticipation. Children waving at the herculean pets as they ran by. Excited just to see a horse. To win or lose. To be alive.

5

The Hammer's pool was sanitized with Baquacil - a witches' potion that was supposedly a healthy alternative to chlorine. It was the new "hot item" on the pool market, and a few bold customers had paid for the upgrade.

Frankie threw the clipboard at the steering wheel. "Fuck Baquacil, bro. It grows algae faster than a fish tank."

"Should I get the vacuuming equipment?"

"Let's see how bad it is first."

"I thought we were just here to patch a hole. In and out."

"We are. But you can smell the pool from the front yard. He's going to want us to fix it."

"I told you I couldn't lose," I smiled. "Get that $20 ready."

We took one look at the pool and Frankie pulled two $10 bills from his pocket. The water was dehydrated piss yellow. Bulbs of green algae bobbed around like huge Man o' War jellyfish.

It was a horrible sight for eyes singed between sun glare and super weed.

"You could throw a spear in there and catch dinner," I said.

A man pushed through the back door of the house. A tan man. From his figure, I knew he had to be The Hammer. He had the body of a late-night infomercial. The ones from the 80's with some bozo sitting on a workout bench saying, "You'll look like Rambo if you use the 'Ab Cannon' for just ten minutes a day."

"Frankie," he whined, "I paid $2,000 to upgrade my pool and it looks like the punch bowl at a frat party."

"We'll get it clean," Frankie said. "It's the Baquacil.

There's no controlling it."

The Hammer squinted at his pool. Too many hours in the tanning bed had charred his skin. When his temples pressed together his wrinkles and crow's feet looked highlighted with a White-Out pen. "They promised me I'd never have to touch my pool again."

"Well, that's why the big dogs are here," Frankie said to him. Then he put his hand on my shoulder and said, "Go get six bags of shock. We're going to napalm this pool."

I walked across the front yard and felt the daggers of crabgrass stabbing through my flip flops. I looked down at the dried weeds. They gave the yard a nice golden hue. I wondered what it felt like to stand on the high plains of Kansas. Was there a farmer out there with eyes like mine, gazing over his crop, taking it all in?

A small knot formed in my intestinal tract. I leaned against a tree to let it pass.

"Hurry up with the shock," Frankie said.

My stomach started to bubble and twist. I tried to ignore the pain, but it got worse. There was a little demon in my gut, dragging a hot poker around. I thought about all the food and booze I'd consumed throughout the day. It was amazing I hadn't exploded already.

"Frankie," I said. "I need help in the truck."

"What are you looking for?"

"A bucket."

"For what?"

"I've got to shit like a crazy bear."

Frankie went into The Hammer's shed. I heard a loud crash and then what sounded like the N-word. Then he came out with a bucket and ran over to me.

"Don't be shy, bro," he said. "Everyone shits."

"I really don't want the whole neighborhood knowing I have to evacuate every particle of filth from my ass."

Frankie opened the passenger side door of the truck. He put the bucket down on the floor and pulled a box of trash bags from behind the seat. "If you don't do this right," he warned, "we're going to have a tragedy on our hands."

He folded one of the trash bags around the rim of the bucket. Then he pushed down the middle to give a wide opening. "You've got to put your knees on the seat and face the back. Grip the headrest and hang your ass over the edge of the seat."

The side windows of our truck were dirty enough to curtain me off. That didn't make me feel much better, though.

"I feel like dirt scum," I said.

"Don't miss."

I'd read about the public toilets of the Far East. They had foot placement grooves. And right next to your best friend or total stranger you squatted over a hole and let it fly. But here I was in a Jersey suburb, trying to sneak a backwards shit before the housewives watering their gardens realized what the pool boys were doing in this innocent looking truck.

A public poop shack suddenly seemed like the upper end of civilized.

It took me a while to get comfortable. I rolled the window down a crack for ventilation.

"Yo," I heard The Hammer say to Frankie. "Can you get your truck out of the driveway?"

Frankie turned and frowned at the truck. I was pretty sure he could see me.

"My girl's going to be home any minute," The Hammer added. "You know how bitches are."

"Oh yeah," Frankie said. "I sure do."

I scrambled for a handful of napkins and cleaned up the best I could. Then I placed them in the garbage bag and tied it.

Frankie opened the door and looked at me. I sat with the bag in my hand and looked back at him. I felt like a kid whose dad had just caught him masturbating.

"Well?" he asked.

"Mission accomplished."

"Throw the bag in the bed."

I slid the back window open and threw the bag out. Frankie held his shirt around his nose and said, "It smells like dead cat asshole in here."

"I'm surprised I didn't blow out my central nervous system."

He handed me the keys and told me to move the truck. "I'll bring the shock back with me," he said. "I can't deal with your ass for another second."

I backed the truck up into the street and parked in some shade. Then I reached for the pipe to help my stomach settle down.

The weed was already packed in. Anticipation hung thick in the air - every pool was going to be the death of us. It was only reasonable to smoke hard and strong. We were receiving nothing. All the vibrations had gone bad.

6

I'd been drinking a bottle of water at each house. In the span of a normal day that might have been enough. But it was pool season. And I'd sucked down enough tequila and Jack Daniel's to get a ship of pirates across the ocean. I could see my fingers swelling like fat pink olives.

I picked up the old water bottles on the floor and

drank the remains.

As I was locking up the truck a Lexus pulled into the driveway and parked behind the Maseratis. A red-haired goddess in high heels and sweatpants got out. **"Juicy"** was written across the back pockets in stitched lettering but the **I** and **C** were pretty much swallowed by her crack. She waved at me and then walked to the back-yard, and I trailed behind her like a drunk chicken, my head mimicking each bounce of her butt cheeks.

"Stop staring, bro," Frankie said to me. "You're going to creep her out."

The Hammer stepped up for a smooch, but she put her hand on his face and blocked him.

"The pool looks like shit," she said. Then she did a little spin-move in case he forgot what she brought to the table. "You think this shit is free?"

"I wouldn't want it if it was, baby. You know me."

"Yeah, I know you." She kissed his neck. "You're mommy's sexy little bitch."

She went into the house and The Hammer asked Frankie what he thought of his new girl.

"I think ... God bless America," Frankie said.

"That's right. Now stop standing around staring at my girlfriend. We're having important clients over for dinner. I can't have them in a pool that smells like a Red Lobster."

"We'll take care of it."

"Because my girlfriend ... she's not happy."

"We'll take care of it. I promise."

Frankie told me to dump all the shock into the pool. The other pools we had worked on were swim club sized. But The Hammer's was basically a bathtub. Maybe five feet bigger than a Jacuzzi. Six bags of shock would sterilize a woodchuck in the next town.

But what did I care? The Hammer seemed to be getting fresh with Frankie. The shock was subtle payback and it left no evidence. The Hammer would itch and burn, but he wouldn't know why.

"Actually, hold off on the shock," Frankie said. "I think we're going to have to get in the pool."

7

The day was shaping up to set a heat record. Anything that could dig a hole had crawled underground. We still hadn't picked up any sunscreen. I looked at the freckles on my shoulders. They seemed to be molding into one brown cancerous mass.

I was starting to see the events of this day as a montage that had been branded with an X rating. A predetermined course with a script I'd never read but always known. The Sunday nuns had promised us that He was an all-knowing God. They must have understood this also meant there could be no coincidences in life. Somewhere, in that celestial theater of our Lord, He was watching with a beer and a bag of popcorn. Smiling. Knowing it was all playing out exactly the way it should be.

Which was fine, except that it appeared we had a slight difference of opinion as to what constituted good art.

8

My reflection looked at me from the slow current of the pool. White corpuscles were blasting in my eyes like I was staring halfway into a nightmare. I tried to move my head away from the water, but the glare from the sun had an addictive burn.

"Bro, you look like you just had a lobotomy," Frankie said.

The air suddenly felt like a wet blanket that had been microwaved and wrapped around me. I smiled at him, then collapsed into the pool.

I woke up to The Hammer pouring a cup of water on my face. Frankie stood over him, studying me.

"Frankie," I said. "I saw him."

"Saw who?"

"The Devil. He was roasting a pig and laughing with the Queen. He took a knife and cut off one of the pig's ears. I was shaking three dice and rolled them. The first two stopped short. One was four. The other five. But there was nothing to stop the third. It just bounced away. The Devil put his hand on the Queen's head and pushed her down to her knees. She stuck her tongue out and he dangled the pig ear in front of her. Then he traced her lips with it and whispered, 'I wouldn't steer you wrong'."

The Hammer looked at Frankie.

"He had a southern accent," I added.

"Should I call an ambulance?" The Hammer asked.

"Nah," Frankie said. "He says shit like that all the time."

9

The Hammer told us he was "going to make a mess" on his girlfriend's face and went inside. I stood in the shade while everything came back into focus. The vision scared me. Was the Queen my savior, or a soldier of Satan?

Frankie was waist-deep in the pool. He had a small canvas seal in one hand and a can of waterproof glue in the other.

"I need you to stand on my back," he said to me. "I have to go under to patch the hole."

"What if I drown you?"

"I'll bite your ankle if I need air." He put the seal and glue can down on the side of the pool. "Grab the skimmer pole. Stick it against the back of my head and push as hard as you can."

I got the skimmer and climbed into the pool. We did a test run. I pushed down on his skull and balanced on his waist. His face was held firmly against the floor, but the rest of us kept floating up.

"Let's try this a different way," he said. "You get out of the pool and push me down with the skimmer."

He stuck his pinkie into the glue can and swirled it around. Then he scooped out a clear blob and spread it across the seal. "This is the only piece of canvas I have. We have to get it right the first time."

I stood at the edge of the pool and Frankie counted back from three. Then he gave the "okay" sign and went under. I pushed the pole down and held it on his lower back.

The Hammer's girlfriend came out of the house. Her hair was sweaty and stuck to her face. She sat down on a lawn chair and took her top off.

I looked at my bathing suit to manage my situation, then back at her.

The pole started shaking in my hands. I'd completely forgotten about Frankie. He was pounding his fists on the floor and doing a push up motion against the pole.

I let go of the skimmer and jumped into the pool to save him. I hit the water just as he shot up and his head knocked my balls back into my stomach. That pukey feeling started immediately and I doubled over with my mouth open and inhaled about a gallon of the pool.

I heard, "It's just one catastrophe after another with you," as water leaked out of my eyes and nose. Then he said, "Well, what the hell, man? You almost killed me."

I wiped my nose and spit out some water. Then I cupped my hand around my mouth and whispered, "I've got a surprise for you."

"What?" he asked.

"Look around."

I watched his eyes go from tight and angry to full headlights as he realized a beautiful rack was hanging out ten feet from us.

"Whoa. Nice, bro."

I stuck my fist out. "Wake and bake?"

"Yes, sir. Wake and bake."

10

The Hammer's girlfriend didn't appreciate the attention. After our fist bump she got up and went inside. She gave us a look like it was our fault for staring.

"See that?" I said. "Everyone gets all uncomfortable when they realize the slaves are people too."

"She can take her boobs and fuck off," Frankie said. "The Hammer has a new girl here every week."

"I hate to say it, Frankie, but I think we might be in the wrong line of work."

"Why do you think I've been doing so many sit ups?"

I decided to do at least ten crunches at the next pool. But by the time we got in the truck I'd smoked another dozen cigarettes and thought it best to start tomorrow.

CHAPTER FOURTEEN

Weekly #3

1

We stopped at a Wawa on our way to the next pool. It was coffee time. Any energy from the sliders had worn off long ago. Frankie talked about taking a vacation to Hawaii. All I could do was grunt. I was heat-stroked and full of alcohol; burnt out on weed and my second coffee crash.

I looked at my friend. He did this every summer. Every year. And I never heard him complain.

I asked him how.

"Because I'm Frankie Gunnz," he said. "Nobody's better."

2

I was still pretty drunk when we got to the next house. The thought of having to leave the truck and do more work was unbearable. I looked up and saw the sky littered with chemtrails. As if a thousand rockets had been launched from every corner of the horizon and a giant Tic-Tac-Toe board was being chalked onto the pitiless blue.

It's all bad, I thought. From top to bottom.

And it got worse.

The next pool was surrounded by a wall of poison ivy. The vine slithered around every post and branch in the backyard like an infected tree snake.

"This is some sincere savage evil," I said when we got to the backyard. "I can't even see the pool through all the poison ivy."

"When I get a house I'm growing plants around it just like this," Frankie said. "I already know I'm going to hate my neighbors."

The lavender leaves of ivy were blocking the sun from touching the ground. A permanent shadow hung over the backyard like something unholy had moved in.

"Frankie, I'm allergic. I may die from even looking at it."

"Then cover your eyes. Because we're going in."

There was a pool somewhere, the clipboard said *that* much. But poison ivy is called an "edge plant" for a reason. There was a thin line of concrete, then an endless death jungle.

"Maybe it's not poison ivy," Frankie said.

"It's all three leaves. You can see the toxins dripping off like an acid monsoon."

"I thought poison ivy was green?"

"Not when it's this hot. The sun is boiling the leaves. If it rains, anything breathing on this block will get a blister from the runoff."

"What do we do?"

"There's nothing we can do. Nature won."

A woman came out of the house holding an infant.

"It's about time you got here," she said.

I let out a surprised laugh. Frankie leaned in and whispered, "Look at the balls on this broad." It must be some genetic defect *all* customers share, I thought. As soon as they see someone in uniform an urge to throw shit takes over.

"Listen," Frankie said to her, "I don't know if I can get poison ivy. But today isn't going to be the day I find out."

She rolled her eyes like this was some major inconvenience for her. "I bought some trash bags. I figured you would say something like that." Then she showed us a box of black garbage bags and said, "They're industrial strength."

"What are we supposed to do with them?" I asked.

"Can't you guys tape them around each other?"

She said it like it was the obvious solution. And she looked harmless, but we knew better than to trust anyone. Good intentions usually led to nothing but trouble.

"What do you think?" Frankie asked me.

"I'm no botanist, but plastic would probably work."

"Should I go for it?"

"Hell no. Even the birds keep a distance."

Poison ivy itched worse than falling into an ant hill covered in barbeque sauce. And you never realized that you'd touched it until *after* you had scratched your groin all day.

3

I wrapped half the box of black bags around Frankie. He took the lid off a garbage can to use as a battering ram.

"How does he look?" I asked the woman.

"Invincible."

Frankie grabbed a safety pole and beat his way through the bush. A steady low-mumble of curse words got more creative the further he went. "General Custard's Lonely Heart Shit Band," was a good one.

"Bro, I found the diving board," he said after a few minutes. "It's not as bad as I thought."

I gave the woman a questionable thumbs up. "He tends to see the bright side."

A beeping car horn interrupted our conversation. I recognized the aggression of it immediately.

"Is that what I think it is?" Frankie said.

I ran to the front yard and saw a Pool Universe van driving away. I checked the back of our truck to make sure nothing had been stolen. Everything was still there. I went to breathe a sigh of relief but something in the street caught my eye: a can of spray paint was slowly rolling back and forth.

I walked around to the driver's side of the truck.

We'd been tagged:

UR GAY - Pool U.

I went back and Frankie was even deeper into the poison ivy. I could see leaves and vines flying above the shrub-line. He was hacking at it like a lumberjack.

"What was it?" he asked.

"Please, don't go crazy," I said. "They got us. They tagged the truck."

"Who?"

"Those cunts from Pool Universe."

"What did they say?"

"They said we're gay."

I could almost hear the gears in his brain halting in anger. "Get ready for gangbang central!" he said. "Those happy homos are going to look like jittering crackheads when I'm done with them."

Talking him out of it would've been like trying to reason with a silverback. You'd get two to the face for eye contact.

"Frankie," I yelled into the weeds, "calm down or you're going to hurt yourself."

"Fuck that, I'm coming out. Get the truck started. Daddy Warbuck's bloodline is eating poison ivy for dinner."

The woman clutched her baby against her chest and backed away. I don't think anyone had ever threatened so much carnage in front of her before.

"Does he mean that?" she asked me.

"Once he says it he has to do it. Even if he doesn't want to."

A loud cracking sound came through the plant wall. Then the ground shook with a heavy *thud*. It felt like a building had come down and split the earth.

"Frankie?" I said.

Silence.

"You don't have insurance," the woman mumbled to herself. "He can't get hurt here. You'll lose the house."

"Frankie," I said again. "Are you alive?"

He crawled out of the thick with dirt and loose leaves stuck to his face. "Bro, I fell in headfirst. There's poison ivy all over me."

4

I never let optimism cloud reality. Frankie's broken urethra was one thing. They made pills for that. But ancient plants that sweat and shone nothing but killer toxins could not be defeated.

This was the Universe stepping in.

The woman pretended she heard her phone ringing and slipped back inside. Once she was gone, Frankie said, "That was the worst Irish-exit I've ever seen."

"She doesn't want to watch you take off the garbage bag armor. She might feel obligated to help."

"I knew it was a stupid idea. It didn't work at all."

"Will the $120 this hour costs her clear her conscience?"

"Probably."

It took him forever to remove the garbage bags. They had trapped all his sweat and glued to his body like leather pants. When he finally peeled the last one off, he was covered in red hives and coughing like an old dog.

"I'm going to the hospital," he said. "I still can't piss and I'm about to be itchy as hell."

"What about me?"

"This is what I've been training you for. You know what you're doing."

"I've been stoned since 6 a.m. I don't remember anything that's happened today."

"I'm going to call a taxi. I need you to deal with this woman and go do a collection. All the addresses are in the clipboard. I'll try to meet you at the next house."

It was a daunting prospect. I tended to avoid confrontation in favor of baiting bigger men to handle my battles for me.

But here I was. Alone.

At least with Frankie Gunnz behind the wheel some semblance of order existed. Who was I to demand money from someone? This was my first day of real work. Now *I* was the problem. *THE MAN*. No better than the Sheriff of Nottingham.

I protested.

"This is no time for your rage against the machine bullshit," Frankie said.

He called a taxi and walked to the main road to wait for it. Every moment seemed like the right one to quit. What the hell was a good enough reason to stop working?

5

I put a cigarette in my mouth and watched ants crawl around. My plan was to linger for a while. Procrastinate until a natural disaster, maybe.

The woman came back outside with her kid. "Where is the other guy?" she asked me.

Now that Frankie was gone I didn't have to worry about customer service. I exhaled a cloud of smoke into her face and said, "Your piece of shit backyard is eating him alive. He'll send you a bill for the hospital visit."

"WHAT? He can't do that."

"Take it up with the Boss. I'm leaving."

I crossed my arms to show her I was serious. She rolled her tongue around her mouth. I was expecting a fight, but she smiled and said, "Do you want to come inside? You look like you could use a glass of iced tea."

I nodded slowly. She was pretty. A little wear around the eyes but holding up well.

I cut my cigarette and put it behind my ear. "Iced tea sounds pretty good."

6

She held the door open for me and I stepped into her living room. A flat screen TV was propped up on a milk crate, leaning back on a slight angle against the wall. A treadmill obscured the view to the TV from every angle. It was the centerpiece of the room. There were no couches. No pictures on the wall. Even the light coming in through the front window brought gloom.

She put the kid down on the floor and walked to the kitchen.

"Did you just move in?" I asked.

She opened the refrigerator and took out a decanter full of iced tea. "Oh no. I grew up in this house."

I pointed at the treadmill. "I guess you like to exercise?"

"Me?" she sounded shocked. "Never."

She poured the iced tea into a glass and brought it to me. I took a sip and pretended I'd never tasted anything so good.

"It's my secret recipe," she said. "As soon as it touches someone's lips ... they're mine forever."

A single DVD case lay on the floor next to the television. She went over and opened it. Then she popped the disc out and slid it into a DVD player.

A menu screen flashed on the TV. It said: *Dr. Bronner's Magic Soapbox.*

She bent down and tickled the kid's stomach. "Conrad loves *Dr. Bronner's Magic Soapbox.* It's his favorite movie."

"Oh yeah?" I said. "What's the premise?"

"Soap."

I looked at the kitchen sink and saw five hand soaps surrounding it. And two dish soaps. She became very quiet when she realized I was counting. I could feel her eyes burning into the side of my face.

We stood there in a weird silence while I finished my drink. When I handed it back to her I noticed she had a big diamond ring on her finger.

"I think I should leave before your husband comes home," I said.

"Don't worry about him. He's dead. I'll give you the tour."

She took my hand and brought me down a hallway. We passed three empty rooms. All the same dull prison color of spackling paste.

I squeezed her hand a little. "That's a real shame about your kid not having a father."

"No, it's not. He burned all our savings on Oxy-Contins. I found him overdosing in our bed."

"It's the new American pastime. I'm sorry to hear that."

"Don't be. I went to check my e-mail. Then I watched *The Daily Show*. He was dead when it was over so I called an ambulance."

She brought me into a room and sat me down on a bed.

I presumed *the deathbed*.

There were no decorations in this room, either. Just a little garbage can full of empty gin bottles, and a few half-drunk bottles stacked around it.

"I don't even know your name," I said.

"Isn't that the way you kids like it?"

She was waiting for me to make a move, but I couldn't. It was about the least turned on I'd ever been.

"Do you have a job?" I asked, trying to avoid the inevitable.

"Of course I have a job. You're not looking at some deadbeat welfare mom."

"What do you do?"

She laughed. "I'm a kindergarten teacher." Then she kicked some of the bottles out of the way like she'd forgotten they were there. They were plastic and bounced under the bed.

"Shouldn't we check on your kid?"

Her smile dropped. "He's fine."

I lit the cigarette I had cut outside. I wasn't sure what to say so I just kept trying to avoid eye contact.

"Okay," she said, "I'm going to wash up. Don't you go and run away on me."

She took her index finger and tapped me on the nose with it.

I picked up a gin bottle that still had some liquid in it. I thought about it but decided not to take a swig. Life is tough on women. They spend their entire lives being told to act like something they aren't. And we spend it all trying to find one that's different so we can make her the same. I didn't want to make this lady feel any worse, and I knew what I could do to make her feel good.

I heard sink water from the hallway. A toilet flushed almost the same time the sink started.

Frankie sure was wrong about being a pool boy, I thought. He's never going to believe this one.

The blanket on the bed was made but I didn't untuck it. I couldn't stop thinking about her husband's dead body lying just beneath it.

She came back into the room with lipstick on and shiny hair. I opened the gin bottle and dropped my cigarette in.

"How do you want it?" she asked.

The kid started crying from the living room.

"Conrad, shut up," she said. "Mommy's just talking with her new friend."

He didn't stop. Short screeches of "MA" continued in an endless loop.

Her lips began to quiver.

"Conrad, please. Please. Please. Shut up," she begged.

I couldn't do it. I put my hand on her shoulder. "I can tell you're a great mother. And you're all the right kinds of crazy. But I'm in love with someone else."

She looked at me and her eyes were wild with desperation - the crying eyes of someone about to give up.

"No one has to know," she pleaded.

"I would know. She's my Queen. I just can't do that to her."

Conrad kept screaming like he was being murdered. She buried her head into my chest and said, "Sometimes I just want to hold a pillow over his face. You know?"

"The experiment failed. You'd probably be doing him a favor."

She stopped crying and pushed my hair back behind my ears. "Maybe you should give me your number ... just in case."

I gave her a fake.

"I'll call you now. So you have mine."

"My phone's dead," I lied. "Surprise me sometime."

We went back to the living room and the baby was hitting his fists against the floor. We stepped over him and I thanked her for the iced tea. She leaned in to kiss me but I stuck my hand out and gave hers a shake.

Conrad's screams didn't quit as I walked to the truck. Frankie had taped a piece of cardboard over Pool Universe's graffiti. I ran my hand over the tape to smooth it out.

At least it's never boring, I thought.

CHAPTER FIFTEEN

1

I'd never driven anything bigger than a Toyota Camry. The axle of the pool truck was so banged up that if you were behind it, you'd swear it was driving sideways.

I noticed earlier this created a one-eighty blind spot.

I climbed in and clicked on the hazards. If I hit something now it wouldn't be my fault, I reasoned. I was giving fair warning.

Backing out of the driveway was easy. Before Frankie left he'd said to me, "You always have to remember ... wide turns." I thought about that as I pulled up to an intersection.

Cars were parked on both sides of the road. I took the turn wide, but not wide enough. The truck clipped at least two side-view mirrors clean off. Stopping to assess the situation would have been an admission of guilt.

I didn't even look in the rearview.

After I'd put some distance between me and the cars I picked up the clipboard to find the next address. There was a roadmap taped to the back with a big black circle around the house.

The route brought me past Monmouth Park Race-track. There really wasn't time to get involved with a race, but it *was* the day of the Preakness. I'd lost $100 two weeks ago betting what I thought would be a sure thing in the Kentucky Derby. It would've been nice to make some of that back.

Don't do it, I thought, you're a mush with no money and a terrible record. It was true. I was a schlimazel in every sense of the word. I'd lost almost every race I'd ever bet on, every election I'd ever voted in. On trips to Atlantic City friends made me leave the casino floor before they threw any money on the table.

I hit a red light across from the track. I tried not to look at it but all I could think about was the straight Cee-lo I'd rolled two nights ago with Queen Jac. That girl was more of a long shot than any horse I'd ever bet on, and I won.

I pressed the dashboard ashtray. $8 of singles slid out on a pile of cigarette butts - too strong of a sign to ignore.

I pulled into the poor man's lot. It was about a mile from the front gates of Monmouth Park. I took two singles from the ashtray and handed them to the attendant at the parking booth.

"How's it looking today?" I asked him.

"Just a fine day for a race. The sun is shining all the way up to New England."

"Do you have a newspaper?"

He handed me a copy of the *New York Post*. The idiots who wrote the paper couldn't even be trusted with a weather report, but it would have to do. Frankie had won the lottery after reading his horoscope. I decided to give mine a shot:

Luck will improve and so will stamina.

"I've seen crazier things work," the attendant said. "But betting off of a horoscope seems pretty risky."

"This isn't a fortune cookie. As far as I can tell it's been right about everything so far."

I joined the rest of the late arrivals. They carried everything necessary for a day at the races: coolers, smokers, strollers, playpens, lawn chairs.

A guy wearing a sombrero had a suckling pig draped over his shoulders. Flies hovered around him. The pig was pink like baby fat. Loose drops of condensation rolled down its back. "We've got to get this thing to room temperature," he shouted at his wife. She had three kids on leashes, each one trying to run in a different direction. "You're going to eat this goddamn pig," he said to his kids, "and you're going to like it."

2

Monmouth Park was having its own races all day. The fence of the track was invisible behind a sea of obese, white bodies. Animals roaring at other animals. Sort of like the Roman coliseums but without the dignity. If anyone did anything but stand and sit they'd immediately fall into diabetic shock. I watched a guy hand a seagull his empty bag of chips so he wouldn't have to get up and walk to a garbage can.

Magazines were handed out at the gates with the names of the horses racing and each of their stats. I flipped through until I found the roster for the Triple Crown race.

Each horse gets a few words about their last performance: usually something about their start, if they broke late, how many lengths behind the lead, how they handled the bend into the stretch, if they ran out of gas in the final furlong. Most people bet on what name they like best, but if you follow the stats down the line it gets a little easier to finger the horses taking the top three positions.

Inside the grandstand you find the real miscarriages of humanity. Men who've been to the track so many times the actual action doesn't even turn them on. Men who couldn't remember the last time they had seen the track's dirt glow red under the bottom of the sun. They sit on stools and hunch over the books. Circling schemes. Mouthing cut cigars. Rags constantly dabbing at the sweat pouring down their faces. Always one race away. They get up to take a piss. Drink more of the beat coffee. Shovel down a few hotdogs. And sit again until the night calls, sending them back to whatever doghouse they crawled out of.

I always took the route through the grandstand but never bet there. It just seemed cursed with the death of fortunes and hopes of decent men.

But this scene which might enter your mind as tragic hangs in your memory like a shiny ornament when the exit doors open. Because they swing left and right. You step out with your pockets still fat and the day looks drowsy in all the right ways. It spits at you with all of its warmth. You watch a father pour sloppy shots into red solo cups. His friends pick them up and hold them toward the sky. He winks at his woman and recites a speech to his tribe: "Let the cigars be fresh, scores be low, steak be bloody, the scotch be old, cards come fast and beers be cold." When you look back on something this charming you find that your definition of satisfaction has been played with, and exceeded.

There were computers for betting on every path but I never used them. For a sport based on the brutal heart of a living thing, figuring out a math-machine seemed out of place. Boxing. Trifectas. Boxed Trifectas. Better to find a human you could blame when it all went wrong.

I walked into a betting booth. TVs lined its walls with races from Abu Dhabi to Berkeley. I had Frankie's $20 from The Hammer's pool, $4 left from my father, and $6 left from what I'd found in the truck. I handed the wad of cash to an attendant and told her I wanted to bet the Preakness.

She smoothed out the bills against the corner of her desk and said, "When a horse breaks its leg out there they put it down without even seeing if it can be rehabbed. But that's the price of being born with a purpose."

"To be so lucky."

I didn't have the kind of cash you needed to bet a horse with good odds. Even if my $30 bet won the payout wouldn't be enough for a carton of cigarettes. So I took the horse with the worst odds: Northern Giant, 30-1.

I said a prayer while she printed out my ticket. Then I walked back to the truck.

3

I needed someone to keep me updated on the race.

Lunchbox had a bookie cousin somewhere in North Jersey. I knew he'd be at home watching because he bet anything his cousin would extend him credit for. And Lunchbox wasn't like me. He always won.

I went through the contact list on my phone to see if there was anyone else I could text.

He had gotten to the Queen first.

But obviously there wasn't going to be anyone else. Twenty million people watched the race every year and somehow the only one of them I knew had already slept with my dream girl.

I went through again - just in case - then I sent him a text and asked him to alert me when the race had a winner.

The parking attendant told me this year's Triple Crown was anyone's prize. The Kentucky Derby had just been declared "the most wide open in years" and today's Preakness didn't have any strong favorites.

"You can be on your way to retirement," he said to me. "Just don't forget the little guy."

CHAPTER SIXTEEN

Collection #1

1

Three old muscle cars were rotting in the driveway of the next stop. Which meant I couldn't park in it, like Frankie always did. I rolled the window down and didn't hear any cursing, so I figured Frankie probably hadn't arrived yet. Which meant I could do nothing for a little while longer.

I parked in the street and counted hours of work on my fingers. I was into the eleventh. The seat reclined a bit with my slouch. It took some effort, but I managed to lift my arm and turn on the radio. An expert whose name I'd never heard was quoting a source he couldn't mention: "The bottom line is - The Empire is in full collapse," he announced. "Will THEY show us mercy when we're on the other end of the gun barrel?"

I turned down the radio and studied the house. It had disaster written all over it. Another ranch in a development of cloned ranches. Every house in competition to fly a bigger American flag than the one next door.

Except mine. The house I was going to had no flag, no 9/11 memorial, not even a statue of The Virgin Mary, and bare of these things it looked almost threatening.

I'm surprised no one has called the FBI yet, I thought. I can't wait to meet the mongoloid that lives here.

A chicken wire fence ran the length of the backyard, standing about head high. Little white casings were impaled by the pickets of the fence but I couldn't tell what they were. New Jersey wasn't much different than the old west. Unless you were a Girl Scout mother the high rule never changed: Mind your own business.

And here I was, about to break that unwritten law.

I got out of the truck and cracked my knuckles. A kind of tingling was growing stronger in my stomach. Like the feeling right before a first date. The knowing that something wonderful or horrible might be about to happen. And often both do. Usually in that order.

I locked the doors and walked up the driveway to the backyard. As I got closer, I could see those little white casings on the fence were skulls. Animal skulls. Skinned and bleached. They had long jawbones. A few fangs.

The suburbs really are the worst, I thought. Every house is just a box full of weirdness collecting more demons anytime someone walks through the door.

I stuck my face against the window of each muscle car. I was hoping to see something safe, like a stack of Jimmy Buffet CDs, but all their interiors had been stripped away. And the paint had been chipped or sanded off the frames. The only marker on any of the cars was a bumper sticker on the last one. It said:

Better To Have A Gun And Not Need It.

I knew then that I was standing on the lawn of a serial killer, or at least someone ready for a last stand. The scrubbed cars were clearly someone's attempt at cleaning up forensics.

Better to have one and not need it, I thought.

No action had come from the house yet so I went back to the truck and opened the toolbox. Ralph's gun was still hidden at the bottom. I slid both hands under it like it was a baby and laid it on top of the other tools. For a quick draw.

Then I questioned if what I was doing was insane. I looked around for a sign. About a thousand crows were sitting silently in the tree above me. Their eyes watched me with a reptilian gaze.

Better to have one, I thought.

I picked up the toolbox and decided a perimeter sweep was the best way to start. A big blue garbage can was leaning against the chicken wire. I walked toward it and wondered what animals the impaled skulls had come from. They didn't look like anything I'd ever seen in my backyard.

I climbed up on the garbage can and tried to balance on the edges of the lid. It started to wobble just as a man's voice came from behind me shouting, "It's too late!"

The lid slid off like a skimboard and I dropped straight into the can. The toolbox crashed down next to me, hitting the ground corner first, and both hinges snapped off and took the top with it.

The force launched the gun out in a cartwheel rotation. I tipped the garbage can over and crawled out, hugging the ground, waiting for the shot. But it didn't go off. It landed a few feet away with the barrel pointed right at me.

You're going to church all day tomorrow, I thought. You're becoming a priest.

I used my foot to push the gun behind the garbage can before whoever yelled at me got close enough to see. I had my back to him and a huge shadow fell over me like a yeti was standing between me and the sun.

"It's too late," he said again.

He knows I'm onto him, I thought. He probably saw me inspecting those muscle cars. I'll be killed and eaten before Frankie can put the pieces together.

I accepted this fate and tucked my knees into my chest while garbage juice soaked into my butt. I never even turned around to see if I could take him. Giving up seemed like the only noble thing left to do.

"I can't pay you," the man said. "The bank took the house. I moved to this country sixty years ago and I've been broke ever since."

I had to crane my neck to see around his beer gut. It hung over a pair of white Hanes briefs like a whale caught in a fishing net. That was it: all flab, no clothes. Just walking around like this in the middle of the afternoon.

"Sure," I whispered. "Nobody's here to make you do something you don't want to do."

I stood up and wet grime trickled down my leg.

"My name is Karl," he stretched out his hand. "I'm Frankie Gunnz's favorite customer."

He had a faint hint of a German accent, and I could feel his foreign roots as he shook my hand with a limp grip. Had no one ever told him that a solid handshake says a lot about a man in America?

"Frankie loves all his customers equally," I said.

I picked up the top of the toolbox and started collecting everything that had fallen out.

"I had that toolbox once," Karl said. "Another cheap Chinese hunk of junk. It practically broke before I was out of the Home Depot."

"We're like prisoners building bullets for the enemy."

He picked up a hammer I'd missed and handed it to me. "No one's better at Capitalism than the Communists."

"You're the second Carl I've met today," I said. "Isn't that weird?"

"My name is Karl with a 'K'. You're saying it with a 'C'."

"How can you tell?"

"I invented telepathic transmission. Then I invented autism to make my job easier." He chuckled like he had just let me in on some good gossip.

"Well, the other Carl was a major pissfart. Maybe you can telepathically drop cancer on him."

"I wish I could drop that on everyone. While I've got you here would you mind looking at the pool? It's been green for a month."

"How much?"

"How much what?"

"Do you think I'm a pool boy because I felt a calling to this kind of work? If I'm giving you my time, I need to see some cash ... or flesh."

"In my day you were thankful just to have a job."

"Two nights ago I scored with a girl I'd take an ingrown toenail for. If I get out of here early enough, I'm pretty sure I can make it happen again."

"Now you're talking. How much do you want?"

"Whatever you got. I just blew all my money on the race."

"Preakness?"

"Yes, sir."

"Who'd you take?"

"Northern Giant."

"Ouch."

"I know."

"I guess if you're not going to bet first, bet last."

"I've got Manny Pacquiao for $300 next month. I'd like to throw some more on him."

"You can never put enough on Pacquiao. He's the only guarantee there is."

We nodded at each other.

"Let me put the toolbox back in the truck," I said. "Then I'll look at your pool."

"How about this? Put the toolbox back, then come in and watch the race. I took Lookin' At Lucky. If I win, I'll throw you some cash. You can look at the pool when it's over."

We shook again. I was like one of those short-selling stockbroker scumbags, an entrepreneur with real grit, taking paper away from those who didn't have any, and not feeling guilty at all.

2

Karl leaned against the fence and watched me while I put the toolbox away. He patted his gut back and forth with each hand like he was slapping out dough. His body was so gross and pathetic I started to think that maybe he wasn't a murderous psycho. Maybe he just collected old cars, liked guns, didn't care about the societal contract of 'fitting in.' I could see a life like this - no woman, no pain, get fat, get drunk, only wear underwear. Recline right into the good years, get forgotten the minute after you're dead.

Of course, it was this same sort of charm that got thirty people buried under John Wayne Gacy's house.

Karl put his arm around my shoulder and led me into the backyard. A paintball gun was sitting on a little table. He picked it up and pointed it at three cardboard cutouts of Domino's pizza boys. They were dripping with fresh paint splatters.

"Target practice," he said. Then he squeezed the trigger and every color of the rainbow exploded against the pizza boys.

He put the gun down and admired his accuracy. "Not bad for an old man, huh?"

A cardboard gorilla stood a few feet away from the pizza boys. It hadn't been defaced with paint like the others.

"What's that one?" I asked.

"That is one damn dirty ape."

"It looks like it's going to come and bite us."

"No, that's Adam. Adam's a good boy. He's there as a reminder."

"A reminder of what?"

"No matter how many backyards a forest can be cut up into, we're all still the beasts we came from."

3

Karl opened a back door and we entered a bedroom. A circle-shaped waterbed took up most of it.

"Take a seat on the waterbed," he said.

The bed was the only place to sit. A bunch of black silk pillows lay on black silk sheets.

"Do you like those sheets?" he asked. "They were all I was able to take with me when I left the Rhineland."

I took inventory of the room. Crates full of yellowed newspapers surrounded the bed. I could read the first headline of each stack. I saw ones about the Kennedy assassination, a Fort Detrick experiment, and a couple about Waco.

Karl fumbled around on a bar cart and handed me a dirty martini. Then he turned on a black and white TV, but it was all fuzz. A mangled set of rabbit-ear antennas stuck out from the back. He bent them around until we got a view of the race.

There was still some time left. I asked Karl for his bathroom.

He laughed at me in a tone more soulless than a hollow statue. Then he pointed down a hallway and said, "I hope you're not scared of mannequins."

I laughed back, knowing I'd probably never see the outside world again. Karl was either a genius or a cannibal. And either one was capable of turning me into a lampshade.

I pushed doors open as I walked down the hallway. I wanted to make sure there were no children chained up, but nothing was out of the ordinary.

Maybe I'm judging this guy too quickly, I thought. It's not his fault he's lonely.

I opened the bathroom door and a man was sitting on the toilet.

"Holy shit," I said. "I didn't know anyone else was here."

He didn't move.

"You're not a person, are you?"

I was talking to a life-sized mannequin dressed in a black Nazi uniform. An S.S. General's hat rested on its head. The outstretched wings of a silver eagle flew proudly above the brim. I leaned forward and read the name tag pinned into its chest: *Hans.*

The Nazi doll made me shiver. It felt like a crime, being in its presence.

Don't be rude, I said to myself. Just watch the race. Finish your drink. Say thank you. Then walk to the truck and drive far away.

I lifted Hans and put him on the floor. He'd been blocking a paperback copy of *The Brothers Karamazov* sitting on the toilet tank. It was opened about halfway, face up.

Strange literature for a fascist, I thought.

I read the back cover while I finished pissing. Then I flipped it over and read a line on the page it was opened to:

"In most cases, people, even wicked people, are far more naive and simple-hearted than one generally assumes. And so are we."

"That's really good writing," I said to Hans. "The wise man knows he knows nothing."

I washed up and put Hans back on the toilet. Then I grabbed the book and walked to the living room as if I encountered this sort of lunacy all the time.

"Did you meet Hans?" Karl asked.

"Yeah." I held up the book. "Do you mind if I borrow this?"

"Will you bring it back?"

"Sure."

"That's what everyone says."

He pat the bed. Rolls of water rose and sank as if the sheets were being caressed by an invisible hand.

I didn't move.

"Come sit down. The race is about to begin."

The doorbell rang, interrupting our stalemate.

Karl rolled off the bed and hit the floor hard. "Get down, kid. Don't let them see you."

He stretched his big toe to the TV and poked the volume button until the sound went off. Then he crawled to a window and peeked through the curtain.

This is your chance, I thought. Run.

I went to another window and tried to lift it. A nail in the frame kept it from moving more than an inch. Every muscle in my body sagged. I did the sign of the cross.

Karl got up and opened the door. "Come on in, Frankie," I heard him say. "The race is about to begin."

Frankie strolled in like his name was on the mortgage. He didn't even seem concerned that Karl was hanging out with me in his underwear.

The three of us sat on the waterbed. We watched the race and Frankie got an earful of how the bank stole the house.

Lookin' At Lucky won and Karl gave me $5. I thanked him and we stood up to leave.

"What about the pool?" he asked.

"I told you last time," Frankie said. "Throw some goldfish in it. They'll eat the mosquitoes."

4

Frankie and I got back into the truck and stared ahead for a long time.

"I feel like I just got molested," I said.

"And that's not even the worst part. That degenerate didn't have any of the money he owes the Boss. Now we're going to get yelled at."

I slapped myself in the forehead. "I forgot the gun."

"What gun?"

There were only a few days between garbage pick-ups. The gun wouldn't be lying around for *that* long. Even if Karl found it early, everything I'd ever read said most incidents with firearms were self-inflicted.

Maybe he'd take it as a sign from God. A final act of repentance. And there's no honor in discouraging Nazi suicide, I thought.

"No gun," I said. "I'm hallucinating again. Let's get out of here."

CHAPTER SEVENTEEN

Weekly #4

1

My phone started singing. It was a text from Lunchbox: *Lookin' At Lucky took the gold.*

Just seeing his name was beginning to pinch a nerve.

"Lunchbox is a real dick," I said to Frankie.

"That guy's got his name on every girl's list. Lucky bastard."

I pictured him and the Queen running around that shore town during Senior Week. Playing skeeball. Riding the Ferris wheel together. Watching those Ferris wheel lights paint the Jersey waves.

It's all right, I thought, you've had fun too. It's the growing flower of a young woman - pruned by many suitors until finally plucked and placed in the vase of the special *one*.

Or so they said.

I actually hadn't had any fun. I'd followed the rules for too long, always waiting in line to find my place while everyone else just enjoyed the ride.

And I'd finally gotten her. I'd proved my worth beyond all the others. And my stupid brain wouldn't even let me enjoy it; it was on a mission to sabotage my heart.

"The doctor said I'm immune to poison ivy," Frankie said.

"How's the penis?"

"Ain't like it used to be, that's for sure."

"Did they castrate you?"

"I have another UTI," he frowned. "They gave me some pills so I can start pissing again."

"At least there's a Democrat in The House. You'll hang onto your health insurance for a few more years."

The dusty day was beginning to settle into an opiated afternoon. Everything was silent. Even the wind was too lethargic to move. Tree limbs dangled south, impotent and pathetic.

"Three more," Frankie said. "Just three more."

2

A cool wind brought wispy clouds in from the shore. An ethereal hand with a feather dipped in white paint was brushing over the sky's deep blues. Like sidewinder trails in the sand.

We sat in the driveway of our fourth weekly and finished old cups of coffee.

"Let's bang this one out fast," Frankie said. "It feels like it's about to start raining."

There weren't any trees so the vacuuming job would be light. I pulled the pump and the filter out of the truck. The pump clipped the scab off my shin and some fresh blood started flowing. Frankie stood behind his open door and tried pissing into an empty water bottle.

I left him at the truck and carried the equipment into

the backyard, dripping blood across the patio.

Two teenage girls were sunning themselves by the pool. One blonde. One redhead. The blonde wore a zebra bikini that fit like an eye patch. The redhead was in a leopard bikini that crisscrossed in small bands up her stomach.

Frankie came through the gate. "That's trouble."

"Finally."

"Wake and bake?"

"Wake and bake."

Frankie got down and did a set of pushups. His tan had turned into a nice bronze at some point during the day.

I looked at the girls.

They noticed.

I started vacuuming and pushed it in their direction. The girls never looked at me, but each time Frankie lifted up and exhaled down they shook with excitement.

To be young and stupid. To be desired by the young and stupid.

I'd take either.

They passed a water bottle full of yellow liquid back and forth. The blonde arched her spine and stuck her chest out when she realized I was listening to their conversation.

"You should see his O-face," the blonde said.

"I hated his O-face," the redhead said. "I always looked away."

"Not me. I get right in his face and stare as hard as I can. It freaks him out."

What a sinister duo, I thought. Years from now they'll still be sitting right here, faces full of wrinkles, wondering where all the good men have gone.

"I think the O-face is God's joke on humanity," I

said to them.

The blonde grabbed her towel and pulled it over her breasts. The redhead raised one side of her lip and looked like she might spit at me.

You sound like a pedophile, I thought. Even horny sixteen-year-olds are repulsed by you.

I went over to the heater box and relayed the story to Frankie. He looked back at the girls and said, "Don't feel bad. If you never had *it* you can't lose *it*."

"Sometimes I forget and I think I have *it*."

"That's how people get into trouble."

He scratched his chin like a sensei in deep thought. Then he snapped his fingers and said, "There's this book called *The Art of War* my dad used to keep in the bathroom. You ever read it?"

"No."

"I only read one page but it taught me this: there are people who want steak, so they sit at the table and take a steak. There are other people who want steak but for some reason they're afraid to take it. They know if they wait under the table and sniff around long enough eventually someone will feel bad and throw them a scrap. But when they get it, instead of demanding more, they run away with their small piece and hide somewhere while they eat it. The thing about the second team is they've convinced themselves they're equal to the first. That earning it is somehow as honorable as just taking it. And then there's the King. He always sits at the head of the table."

"Which team am I on?"

"Not mine."

3

I packed up while Frankie poured shock into the pool. When he walked back to the truck, I handed him the clipboard and grinned.

"What?" he asked.

"Those girls ..." I sighed. "If only I'd known then what I know now."

"I knew it then. It didn't make any difference."

"It's too bad Ralph isn't here. I'd love to set him loose on a couple of young chicks."

We got into the truck. Frankie rifled through the papers on the clipboard to see what was next.

"It's a good thing Ralph blew himself up," he said. "We've got Igor next."

"Sounds like another asshole."

"You'll like him. He's a crazy Russian. Hates cops."

"We should take his lead. Russians usually aren't wrong."

"I think their graveyards would disagree."

I pulled *The Brothers Karamazov* out of the glovebox. The translator's note began with a letter Dostoevsky had written to his brother.

I read the passage to Frankie:

"Man is a mystery: if you spend your entire life trying to puzzle it out, then do not say that you have wasted your time. I occupy myself with this mystery, because I want to be a man."

I lifted my head.

A moment passed in silence.

"What the hell am I supposed to do with that?" Frankie asked.

"We're going to ask Igor. I suspect he'll know better than us."

"You don't know Igor."

"Well, Frankie, whatever a Russian is doing to live in this part of New Jersey means he's doing it better than us."

Frankie smiled and said nothing else.

CHAPTER EIGHTEEN

Collection #2

1

He was right. I didn't know Igor. Maybe it was because of the two pages of Dostoevsky I had read, but I was picturing a hairy man in a black robe, living in a shelter like some unearthed saint.

Igor was the other kind of Russian.

We parked in front of something my dad would've referred to as a: "Guinea Pavilion." Which meant it looked more like a Las Vegas casino than a house. He used the term pretty liberally, and it was usually followed with: "Who has this kind of money? From Maine to Florida, nothing but wasted money." But as far as gaudy homes went even he would've agreed this one took the cake. Every block of marble in Italy must've been shipped over to build it. Two stories higher than any house in the neighborhood, the neighbors could forget about getting any sun. The perimeter was twinkling with halogen lights like a private UFO airport. And a forest of fake plants filled the front yard and made the whole place smell like a plastic factory.

I put *The Brothers Karamazov* back into the glovebox. "You were right," I said. "I don't think Igor is going to reveal the mystery of man."

"This is why they shouldn't make kids read," Frankie said. "How could you not end up disappointed with everything?"

I was in the vortex of the new American Dream; a place for Nazis and Russian mobsters to get a fresh start with an old-world ethic. They were now free to live in a land dumbed to reality TV levels, arriving with wallets full of cash that found favorable conversion, and a national creed that said the past is in the past because all is fair in the pursuit of wealth.

2

This was just a collection so we didn't have to bring anything out of the truck.

"In and out," Frankie said. "Don't get sidetracked."

I followed him to a wood fence. He raised the knuckle of his index finger and did a secret knock: *1-1-2-2-1*.

The fence swung open. A little boy with a baseball glove greeted us with, "Oh ... it's you."

"Is Igor home?" Frankie asked him.

He scanned the yard like he was expecting to see people hiding behind the fake trees. Then he nodded and said, "I'll take you to the King."

He led us down a concrete path that wound around the back of the house. Big statues of naked men stood along the sides with their cocks right in our faces.

I laughed.

"Be cool," Frankie said.

We turned a corner and a wall of burning tiki torches blocked the rest of the path. The boy pulled one out of the ground and stepped aside, to let us pass.

"You'll find Igor through there," he said.

The flames danced in front of our faces like we were at the gates of Hell, about to be offered up in some Illuminati sacrifice.

"Is this how it ends?" I asked Frankie.

"Don't worry, you're going to be very happy."

He stepped through the tiki torches and disappeared. I took a deep breath and did the same, expecting the worst. But then I saw the pool and stopped.

It was a masterpiece come to life before my eyes.

Water cascaded down slides and spilled like single brush strokes into a heavenly bath. Rings rippled from topless Sirens as they swam, and other girls lounged on big floats like a beautiful spell had been cast on this backyard.

A grotto broke the pool in two. In the shallow end, kids were taking turns tackling each other off the steps into the water. An older, fatter woman was losing her mind trying to keep them from drowning.

Frankie pointed at her. "That's Igor's wife."

I ignored her and looked back at the other girls in the pool. "I'm going in."

I kicked off my flip flops and started walking toward the deep end. Frankie clenched his fist around my shirt and motioned at the only man in the yard; a man in a silver bathrobe with a matching tangle of chest hair.

"That's Igor," he said. "You want to take a chance pissing Igor off?"

Igor was swinging a spatula around, flipping sausages on an open grill. He raised two fingers and did a half-wave to his wife, a thick cigar mashed between them. She nodded back and pulled a little girl out of the pool by her hair. Like a mother cat. The girl didn't even whimper.

No, I thought. You certainly don't want to piss *either* of them off.

Igor's wife toweled off another kid and we all walked together to the grill. Igor looked up and gave us a big smile. "Here he comes, it's Frankie Gunnz," he said with a melody. "Get over here, Gunnz. Eat some food."

Frankie tried to decline, but Igor wrapped his arms around us and pulled us both in for a hug.

We were getting sidetracked.

Igor was about five feet tall. I felt like a giant standing next to him. I glanced down at his head. His hair parted like a bullet had been shot straight down the middle, gelled to each side.

"This is Igor's welcome home party," his wife said to us.

"Welcome home party?" Frankie asked him. "Where've you been?"

"Jail."

"Jail?"

"The bastards nabbed me in Elizabeth. I went to buy some pork and next thing I knew I was in handcuffs. I spent the night in the can before they could get a Judge in to see me."

"What'd they get you for?"

"Moonshining. Can you believe that? They had me in the bullpen with a whole gang coming off PCP." Igor said he went to court and the Judge made him stand right up in front. "The Judge said to me, 'Igor, you have five pots in your backyard.' So I said, 'But Judge, I don't have no still.' Then the Judge said, 'Igor, you've got a coiled copper pipe.' And I told him again, 'But I don't have no still'."

Igor's wife jumped in. "That Judge has had it out for him for years."

Igor gave her a pat on the head, but he let a few seconds pass before he continued his story, like he was giving everyone a warning not to interrupt him again.

"So then the Judge said to me, 'Igor, we've got you on tape buying thirty pounds of cornmeal.' And one more time I told him, 'But Judge, I don't have no still.' He'd had enough by then and said, 'Yes, but you've got all the equipment. You're being fined $5,000'."

Igor said he threw his hands up in the air in defeat. "Finally, I told him, 'Well, Judge, you might as well arrest me for rape, too.' 'Rape?' he yelled at me. 'Did you rape somebody, Igor?' 'No,' I said, 'but I've got all the equipment'."

We all laughed.

Frankie gave Igor a high-five.

"The Judge must have shit himself," Frankie said. "What did he do?"

"He let me go. Leave it to the pigs to arrest me a week before distilling. If they had waited another seven days they could've put me away for a year."

A splash-fight started in the pool. Wet blonde hair began clinging to cheeks and shoulders. I grinned like an idiot. I didn't care.

Igor pinched his wife's fat cheek and said, "This beautiful woman was waiting at the courthouse with the pork I'd been trying to buy."

"Of course I was," she said to us. "Please remind him how lucky he is to have me."

We all laughed again.

Igor slid two sausages onto a plate and handed it to Frankie. "Softest meat in New Jersey," he said.

After a story like that we couldn't say no, so we ate.

And one by one, beautiful half-naked women emerged from the pool and took sausages.

"Can I get a beer?" I asked.

Igor pointed at a cooler. "Cold beer in there. Good vodka inside."

"Igor, if I wasn't on the clock I'd drink all your vodka." I reached into the cooler and took a beer. "You know Frankie, though. He runs a tight ship."

"Same ol' Frankie Gunnz," Igor said. Then he studied Frankie's face for a second. "Nice eyebrows, Frankie. Did you get a girlfriend yet?"

"No."

"Today's your lucky day. Take my new girl. Her name is Masha. She's around here somewhere. She just moved in."

The kid who'd brought us to the tiki torches was tossing a baseball in the air. He was trying to catch it in a glove that had never been oiled.

"Hey, kid," I said. "You're doing that wrong."

Igor stopped serving and squinted at me. He took the cigar out of his mouth and said, "Who are you? Why are you talking to my son?"

"Oh, I'm just his friend," I stepped back, pointing my thumb at Frankie. "Actually, I'm no one. Ignore me."

Frankie repositioned himself to get between Igor and me. "This is Londi. He's a writer. That's why talks too much and gets himself in trouble."

"A writer?" Igor was shocked. "What do you write about?"

"Failure," I said.

"Failure?"

"Yes."

"Perfect. Masha's a pessimist too. She wants to be a writer. I'll introduce you. Give her a talk, all right? Teach her how to make some money so I don't have to pay for everyone around here."

Igor looked back at the kid. The ball left his hand, it went up in the air about the height of the roof, and when it came down it missed his glove and hit him on the shoulder.

Igor shook his head in disappointment. "You know what? Forget about Masha. She's hopeless. Go teach my son how to play baseball."

I had just gotten us sidetracked with a very dangerous man.

Igor shouted over the pool at his son, "Sergey, listen to this guy. He's American. He knows about the baseball."

3

Sergey walked me to the back of the yard. Then he stopped and stared at me with eyes colder than a thousand Russian winters.

"Are you all right?" I asked.

He wound up and threw the ball at me. I caught it with my bare hand. It sent a nerve stabber through my palm, but I ignored the pain.

"Nice try."

I checked to see if Igor was paying attention. He wasn't. I whipped the ball back at the kid. I missed on purpose, but it was close enough to get him face down on the ground, covering his head.

"You want to be a hero?" I said. "Learn to smile when the bullet's coming at you."

He reached under some bushes and dug around. Then he got up with the ball and faced me like he was going to fire it again.

"This ain't the Cold War, kid. Either roll over and give up or kill me this time."

He looked at Igor and thought about it for a second. Then he walked over and handed me the ball.

"Are you this angry at school?" I asked him.

"I hate school. I want to take one of my dad's guns and kill everyone."

"Well, you're never going to grow out of that. But you want to be a baseball player, right?"

"Yeah."

"Then shut up and give me your mitt."

I explained the fundamentals of catching. I tossed the ball up and caught it in a downward motion. Then I brought my right hand down on top of the ball and secured it in the glove.

I did this a few more times.

"Think you've got it?" I asked.

He nodded. I gave the glove back and lobbed the ball into the air. It bounced off his glove.

"You didn't keep your eyes on it," I said.

He handed me the ball and I threw it again. It bounced off his glove, but this time he caught it with his other hand.

"That's right," I said. "That's why your other hand is there."

I threw it once more. He bit his bottom lip and got into position. I could see from his stance that it was going to work. He reached his arms up and caught the ball. A nice clean catch.

I put my elbow around his neck and pulled him into a headlock. Then I dug my knuckles into his skull like a proud coach and said, "See that, kid? It's all in the wrist."

4

Igor handed Frankie a wad of cash wrapped in a rubber band. I lit a cigarette and sipped on a beer. I thought about the house I would own someday. I pictured the Queen drinking from crystal, sitting on a couch above a marble floor.

A blonde came over to me. She looked like all the rest - beautiful and cold. Her face was almost perfectly round. She wore Jackie O sunglasses and an I LOVE NEW YORK t-shirt.

"I'm Masha," she said.

"Londi."

She leaned in and kissed my left cheek. Then she kissed my right cheek. I hated this kind of interaction. Shaking hands was awkward enough.

"Igor told me you're a writer," she said. "I'm a writer too."

"What have you written?"

"Nothing yet. But someday I will."

"Don't bother. You would have done it by now if you were going to."

"Plenty of people write when they're older."

"Who?"

"All the good ones."

"Well, it works out for some."

"I can be a writer."

"Don't you think the world has enough writers? Everyone says they want to be a writer."

"You don't know me. You don't know anything about me."

"I'm not trying to give you a hard time. But the world needs more readers, not writers. Everything there is to say has already been said."

Masha turned around and stomped her way over to

Igor. She was really pissed.

Frankie was leaning into the pool and Igor was explaining something. Masha didn't care. She practically straddled Frankie to get attention. Her arms jerked around in a tantrum and Igor and Frankie turned and looked at me.

Another one who just wants to hear someone tell them they're special, I thought.

I always felt bad for people who never found their thing.

5

"What did you say to Masha?" Igor asked me.

"I told her not to quit her day job."

"Well ... somebody had to do it. Does my boy have the chops? I try and tell him things but he thinks he knows better."

"See for yourself," I said. "And maybe keep your guns locked up until he's out of high school."

Igor exhaled like I'd confirmed a fear he'd been trying to ignore. Then he said, "Sergey is dramatic like his mother. He'll feel some pussy soon and then he won't care about anything."

"My dad used to say: 'It's just boys being boys'."

Igor liked that one. "Cool saying - 'boys being boys'. I am sure that is what Sergey is doing."

He seemed reassured with this conclusion and we watched Sergey throw a baseball up onto the roof. As it rolled down he got into the *ready position*. He caught the first one. Then he threw the ball up and caught it again.

"He's like a puppy who just learned a new trick," Igor said.

"Hey, Sergey," I called to him. "Tell your dad what I

told you."

He held the ball up to show us he had caught it. "It's all in the wrist. It's all in the wrist."

6

Sergey promised to practice every day. He also promised to share the wealth when he went big time.

Igor handed me $50 on the way out.

Good start, I thought.

CHAPTER NINETEEN

Igor's son made me think of all the neighborhood kids running around on this first warm Saturday night. What if one of them found the gun I'd left behind at Karl's house? I tried to think of all the ways it couldn't happen, but I was a worst-case-scenario person, and I usually wasn't wrong.

I hid our half-full pack of cigarettes under my seat. Then I held up an empty pack to show Frankie. "We need to get more cigarettes. I'll use the money Igor gave me."

"Already? Jesus, we must have smoked a thousand today."

Frankie drove us to a Wawa. Luckily, there was one on almost every corner. It was one of the older stores, all gray with the brown duck logo.

"I'll go in," I said. "You relax."

"Take your time. If I can get a five-minute power nap I'll own this world."

I'd once seen Frankie fall asleep standing against a subway pole. I knew he'd be unconscious before I got out of the truck.

I pulled my shirt up over my nose (in case there were any video cameras) and walked to a payphone at the back of the parking lot. I hadn't used one in years and wasn't even sure how to make a call.

I picked up the plastic phone and pressed *9-1-1*.

A dispatcher answered on the first ring.

"9-1-1," she said. "What's your emergency?"

I couldn't think of anything to say. I hadn't expected this to happen so quickly.

"9-1-1," she repeated. "Is this an emergency?"

"I don't know," I whispered. Then I just said Karl's address a bunch of times.

"Sir," she said. "What is at this location?"

"A gun," I said. "There's a big gun behind the garbage can."

"A gun?"

"There might also be a Nazi."

"A Nazi?"

I didn't say anything else.

"Sir, what is your current location? What is your name?"

I hung the phone up and ran back to the truck. I got in and pulled the half-pack of cigarettes from under my seat. Frankie had his head against his window with a long line of drool going from his mouth to his shoulder.

I shook him and said, "Time to motate, Frankie."

He woke up, wiped the drool off his mouth, and used it to straighten his eyebrows. "All right, bro. I'm fully recharged."

"Excellent." I passed him a cigarette. "Let's get the hell out of here."

CHAPTER TWENTY

The Mystery Pool

1

The days of May were becoming heavy and long. It was only a few weeks ago, at the start of spring, that the whole world looked ahead and prayed for just this. The time of year when kids throw out their textbooks and run away from the schoolyards. When fathers stare confidently into barbecue flames with nothing to fear. Winter in the rearview. A beer in the koozie. A return to the good life.

But spring days were for the fortunate ones. Now that I was a proletarian, it was the solace of dark I found myself looking forward to. Only when the sun finally retired could this shift end.

The road took on the slow wind of a river, cutting through the flat land of houses and wildflowers. Geese sat along the edges with yellow goslings, holding them close so their new feathers stayed warm while the short grass cooled beneath them.

The entire suburb was dressed in a clean white.

"SOLD" signs picketed front yards. The economy had found its final stronghold and seemed to be keeping it together.

Frankie pulled up a driveway and parked in the flood of a searchlight. A shallow skin of topsoil covered the yard. Above the front door was a little wooden sign: "Welcome To Our Home." A cardboard stork was taped below it. It held a pink basket in its beak and a word box that read: "Congratulations."

"Another one?" I breathed. "Didn't anyone get the memo? The whole world fell apart. What happened to Generation Zero?"

"If I could afford a house like this I'd have ten kids. And I'd name them all Frankie. And I wouldn't vaccinate any of them."

"Who are these people?"

"They're new customers. Hopefully the pool's not a total disaster."

A man in a tucked pink polo walked out from the backyard. "Thanks so much for coming by," he said to us. "Our baby is getting Christened tomorrow. We promised everyone a pool party after."

I ignored him and went to the back of the truck.

"I've cleaned the pool twice," he continued, "but I just can't get the calcium stains off."

"Do you have a waterfall in your pool?" Frankie asked.

The man shook his head no.

"Get five bags of shock," Frankie said to me. "And hook up the big brush."

I looked at the stork again and wondered about this ridiculous world my parents had forced me into. A place where sex was so taboo adults had to pretend birds delivered babies. Let's see how much they like this kid when it turns sixteen, I thought. When it realizes everything since birth has been one big lie.

For some reason I didn't expect them to throw a party for *that* occasion. The truth is a quiet realization always mourned alone.

2

I met them on a deck overlooking the pool. Frankie was explaining how his mother had converted to Catholicism for his Christening:

"She was a Lutheran," he said. "They're so mixed up they don't even think the Eucharist is part of Jesus' body."

"Imagine hanging on a cross and *that's* the thanks you get?" I said.

The man nodded his head in empathy.

"Do you want something to eat?" he asked me.

"I'm good."

"Drink?"

"No."

He opened a sliding glass door and stepped inside. "I'm going to make sure my wife is comfortable. I'll be right back."

Frankie held his hands out at me when the door closed. "What's your problem?"

"Nothing."

"You're being a dick."

"I'm here to clean a pool. I don't want to be friends with some loser in a polo shirt."

I carried the brush over to the pool and almost stepped on a dog. It was a big male, carrying about a hundred pounds of yellow fur.

"Hey buddy," I said to him. "You're some guard

dog."

He rolled over and put his paws up. I scratched his stomach until all four of his legs were making a running motion. Then I dropped the brush and sat down. The dog's tongue slapped my face like a wet hotdog while I pet him. I couldn't stop laughing, and every time I tried to stand up, his tail beat harder against the grass.

"Washington," a woman said. "Stop licking."

The dog stopped licking.

The man was back, this time with his wife. She wore an apron and low white heels. Her hand was locked in his like it was the first time they had ever touched.

"He'll lick you until his tongue falls off," she said to me. "If you let him."

She kissed her husband and went back inside. He came down from the deck and put his hand on the dog's head.

"What breed is this?" I asked him.

"Labradoodle."

"Never heard of it."

"My wife always wanted a dog. I brought him home the day I asked her to marry me."

I looked at the dumb dog. The pool. The big house. "What am I not getting?"

"About Labradoodles?"

"No. How did you do this?" I moved my head around the yard. "All of this?"

He smiled.

I didn't want to see any more smiling.

He knelt down to Washington and said, "It was pretty easy, actually. All of my friends wanted to be rich. I just wanted to be the best person I could. A regular house. A job that paid enough. And I found a woman who was looking for the exact same things."

"How did you know she wouldn't get bored?"

"I told her I'd never need a second chance. I'd never say, 'I could've been a better lover'."

He gave me a nod and tugged at the dog's collar. "Come on, Washington," he said. "Let's go inside."

3

Up in the dark spaces between branches and leaves, mockingbirds took turns caroling back and forth. They sounded like the soft falsetto of mothers singing their children to sleep - the last sweet song of a tribe safe and sound before the new day came and the fear set back in.

I didn't want to hear the mockingbirds. I didn't want any reminders that there was still beauty left in the world. I could get through work at a steady negative pace. A small hint of hope would just keep me crying for hours.

Frankie walked out from the bushes surrounding the filter box. "Everything looks good back there. Just scrub those stains really hard."

White calcium stains had collected over the tiles in the corners of the pool. I gripped the pole and brushed up and down, but the calcium didn't chip off.

"This is such a bitch," Frankie said. "It only happens when the pH is all out of whack."

He went to the truck for a kit that tested alkalinity in pool water. I dumped a packet of shock over each stain. I scrubbed more. Nothing happened.

Frankie came back with a plastic tube and scooped up some water. Then he dripped a few droplets of clear liquid into it.

"It turned purple," he said. "The water's fine."

"I'm going to have a heart attack brushing this hard. Why won't it come off?"

"It's probably been here for years."

I threw the brush onto the grass and walked up the deck. "I'll let them know it's hopeless. They're going to need an axe to get it off."

I went to the back door. Washington was waiting on the other side. He started licking the glass when he saw me.

"Where are your parents?" I asked him.

His head tilted to each side, trying to understand what I was saying.

"You're an idiot."

He turned and walked away from the door. I cupped my hands around my eyes and looked in. The wife was sitting on the floor, cradling a baby in her arms. She was wearing a robe now. One of her breasts was exposed with the baby attached. Her free hand was stroking its bald head, rocking back and forth with the same rhythm the mockingbirds were singing from the trees.

The husband was sitting on a couch and Washington jumped up next to him. He pulled a carrot from a bag and handed it to the dog.

I watched them until Frankie yelled at me from the pool. "What are you doing?"

I turned around.

"Nothing," I answered. "I think they went to bed."

4

I didn't say anything until we had the truck packed. Frankie took all defeats personally, so I knew us leaving with the calcium stains still there was probably weighing heavy. If I said the wrong thing he'd give me a five-finger sandwich before I could apologize.

"Wasn't that guy the biggest wiener ever?" I asked.

"He looked pretty cool to me. And his wife has an excellent butt."

"I'll bet he hasn't been drunk twice in his life."

"Not everyone wants to live like there's no tomorrow. So what if he's a little corny? He got the dog. The pool. The hot wife. I bet you when they cook together it's like watching a dance."

Maybe the snow globe of a Robert Frost poem existed after all.

I suddenly had a terrible fear that it was just too late for me. And too late was worse than not getting it at all. I'd spent most of the day trying to remind myself that time was always cruel, and judging other people's choices was like burning a cigarette into your arm and expecting them to feel the pain; but it was a yoga I wasn't excelling at. All I knew was that good things usually didn't come without a compromise, and even love letters and mixtapes couldn't undo the horrible things of our past. There were things I'd have to accept if I was going to live happily-ever-after with the Queen. The Universe certainly played favorites with Lunchbox, but the underdog eventually gets his day too. I'd gotten mine. And I remembered that nauseous feeling I'd had two nights ago, when I realized everything was going too good to last.

Why does fate always demand such a high cut? I'd spent all my good years dreaming of one girl, and now that things were rolling, I felt like chum floating through a shark tank.

For a minute it all seemed worthless. Was it astrology? Was I just weak? I knew a man in control didn't have to let the past destroy the future. I thought about Buddy Holly. I thought about songs named after Peggy Sue's and Donna's and Mary Lou's and love that didn't stay trapped in old high school halls. I thought about the people who found a Sunday morning Sudoku partner. The happy families I saw sitting together on blankets every 4th of July. The ones who, given the option, wouldn't go back and do it differently.

I turned around and looked at the house. The stork and the baby didn't seem quite so dumb.

Maybe there isn't *always* a monster at the end of the maze, I thought.

Some people know a good thing when it hits them in the face.

Some people get to build a library together and say, "This is all ours."

5

The guy came out with Washington and thanked us for trying.

"I'm really sorry we let you down," Frankie said to him. "There's nothing I want more for your kid's baptism than a perfect pool."

"There're plenty of people out there with real problems. You can't get worked up over the small things." Police sirens had been corrupting the quiet dusk for a few minutes. He nodded in their direction and said, "Did you guys hear about the gun they just found over the highway?"

"What gun?" I asked.

"It's all over the news. The police got a call to check out a gun sighting. They ended up arresting some old man with closets full of Nazi artifacts."

I could see Frankie's brain connecting the pieces.

"Enjoy your party," I said.

We all shook hands and the guy brought Washington back inside.

"Do I even want to know?" Frankie asked me.

"Definitely not."

6

"They seemed pretty happy with their kid," I said to Frankie. "Maybe it's not *so* bad."

"I've always wanted kids. Too bad I need to deal with a woman to have them."

"That's the hard part. I wonder what kind of mother the Queen would make?"

Frankie switched on the ignition and lit a cigarette.

"Let's go home," he said. "We'll get something to eat on the way."

The last pinks of light were burning out, stretched across the sky like strands of yarn, slowly being dragged away under the wave of night.

Frankie's phone rang.

"Please ... no," he said.

It was the Boss.

"Don't pick up," I begged.

He picked up.

"That's impossible," he said into the phone. "You could've drank that pool water when we left."

Someone had called the Boss and complained. Frankie kept looking at me while he and the Boss cursed back and forth at each other. Demerits were being promised, falling to Frankie from the Boss, and from his looks it was pretty obvious they'd land on me.

Frankie hung up and beat his phone against the steering wheel. "Did you vacuum the pool we were at before Igor's?"

"Which one?"

"The one with the little sluts."

"I think so."

"They said you didn't. Now we have to go back and vacuum it again."

"No."

"Yes."

CHAPTER TWENTY-ONE

1

The Gods of love dropped the curtain. Through their black magic or some grand arithmetic, the arms of the Queen were not going to wrap around me on this scurrilous night. The Universe had doll eyes. Nothing to look behind, just pure dilated darkness.

No! My horoscope had said the opposite:

Luck will improve and so will stamina.

Maybe this was a test.

The entire day had been like living under the wrath of a gypsy curse. Queen Jac had a mother. If she'd been read those same storybooks I had, the ones 100-proof with the promise of love, this could be the test. Of course her heart wouldn't just be *handed* over.

I needed to show the Universe what kind of man I was.

Only then could the Queen really understand our love; right at the start of this yellow spring. The honest and truthful love - telling me all of her stories and hoping none of them sounded ordinary, hoping that I'd never begin to think she wasn't as special as I'd sworn she was that first night. And at the end of each one I would jump up and stutter, trying to say a dozen sentences at once, all ending with, "You're the most interesting girl in the world." And it would always be like that. It would always be like the first time you think, "*Maybe forever starts like this.*" We could spend our lives sleeping like pharaohs because we knew in the mornings we would drink more coffee and write a new scripture. The honest and truthful love that was sure to keep us on our knees like the innocent reaching for an icon. The love that dots the star map back to the place where all music comes from. The love that promises, "There will be someone with you on the other side."

2

We pulled into the driveway like two actors signed on to a failing play.

"Leave everything in the truck," Frankie said. "Let's see what the hell is going on."

He opened the gate for me but I made him go first. The girls were still in their bathing suits by the pool. Drunker now.

"Look who's back," the blonde said to us. "Are you finally going to clean my pool?"

The redhead tucked her fingers into her palm and extended her index and thumb like a gun. She pretended to shoot us and said, "Gina's mom said between the two of you, you don't have half a brain."

"Who's Gina?" I asked.

"I am," the blonde said. "My mom is going to get you both fired."

A sliding door opened and Gina's mom walked out. "Gina, get inside. If your father sees you in that bathing suit, he'll have a fit."

Frankie waited for her to finish shaming her daughter. Then he said, "We just got a call from the Boss. What's wrong with the pool?"

"What's wrong with the pool?" she repeated. "Are you kidding me?"

She pointed at the deep end. We both followed her finger to the water. There was a solid brown log the size of a ketchup bottle floating like a fish on its back.

"What is that?" Frankie asked.

"It's a huge piece of shit."

"Are you sure?"

"I don't know what hillbilly town you two came from," she snarled, "but I'm going to call the cops if that isn't gone by the time I come back out."

She went inside and slammed the door.

Frankie gave me a very suspicious look.

"No, Frankie," I said. "I didn't shit in the pool."

"It just doesn't make sense."

3

We walked to the truck to get the vacuuming equipment once more.

"Hey jabronis," a voice called from the street. "Did you like our present?"

Frankie and I looked down the driveway. Two kids were sitting in a Pool Universe van smiling back at us.

"Did you ... poop in that pool?" I asked.

They collapsed onto each other, laughing like two jackals with no idea of the beast they were about to awaken. "Poop?" the driver laughed harder as he said it.

"Who still says poop?"

"No more bullshit," Frankie said. "You get one more chance to give me the right answer."

"Or else what? What are you going to do about it?" He turned to his partner. "Show him what I did to his mother last night."

The passenger put his palms together against his mouth and blew into them, making a wet fart sound. Then the driver yelled, "Suck it, hoes," and they peeled away.

Frankie jumped into our truck and started reversing down the driveway. I dodged the tires and fell back into the grass. He swung the truck wide out into the street, facing the direction the Pool Universe van was headed, and hung halfway out his window and screamed, "I'M GOING TO NEUTER YOU MUTTS AND SEND YOU BACK TO MUTTSVILLE!"

But then he pushed the throttle from reverse to forward without touching the brake. The transmission clipped and it sounded like every gasket in the engine blew.

I got up and started sprinting to the truck. The wheels were spinning round and round but it wasn't moving. Frankie looked like he was about to cry when something finally caught and the truck lurched forward.

"Just go," I said. "I'll meet up with you."

The Pool Universe van skidded to a stop. Black tread shot like confetti from their braking tires.

Frankie threw our truck into park about ten feet behind them. Then he leaned over the passenger seat and pushed the door open for me. I dove in headfirst and looked up at him. "What are they doing?"

"They think they're outlaws, Londi. But they ain't outlaws."

They revved their engine in a loud roar, trying to taunt us into making the first move. They had the advantage. We couldn't see them through their tinted back windows, but we knew they could see us.

"They're watching," I said. "Show no fear."

"Never."

Their engine revved again. This time longer.

We sat still. No noise from our truck. We were angry enough to kill them and they knew it. No need for theatrics.

"They're about to take off," Frankie said.

I picked up the flask bottle of Jack Daniel's from the floor. I unscrewed it and wiped the rim. "You ready to end this once and for all?"

He looked at the bottle, unsure. "I guess if you're going to be a bear, you might as well be a grizzly."

He took it from me and swallowed what was left of the whiskey. Then he tossed the bottle out the window onto a front yard.

Reverse lights lit up in front of us. The Pool Universe van started rolling backwards.

"What the hell?" Frankie said.

"They're going to crash into us."

Frankie reached through the back window of our truck and stuck his hand in the tool bag. He rummaged around, knocking screwdrivers and plugs out until he said, "Ah-ha," and came up with a white mallet.

The Pool Universe van stopped. A McDonald's bag flew from their driver's window and landed on our hood. The bag ripped at the bottom and French fries spilled out.

Frankie dropped the mallet onto my lap and said, "I'm going to stick a nuke up their ass. El Chapo will look like Mickey Mouse when this is over."

The Pool Universe van took off so fast their exhaust blew the French fries off our hood.

"Get them, Frankie," I said. "Currahee!"

He almost smashed the gas pedal through the floor. But our truck was probably twenty years older than the Pool Universe van. We went after them, but we didn't have the steam to catch up.

"I'm not quitting, bro," Frankie said. "They'll make a mistake eventually."

They stopped again. Packets of ketchup fired from their windows and hit us like bleeding buckshot.

Frankie didn't even slow down this time. He clutched the steering wheel with both hands like he was holding the reins of a war horse.

I picked up the white mallet. "What's this for?"

"When we get close, whack them with the hammer."

They started driving when they realized we weren't stopping. But it was too late. We were even with the back of their van.

"Do it, Londi," Frankie said. "Whack them with the hammer."

I stretched out my window and cocked back. Then I brought the mallet down on their taillight with everything I had. Plastic exploded and ricocheted off of our windshield. Pieces flew in my open window.

They slowed down a little after the hit. They probably would've stopped completely if they weren't afraid of us stomping them into the street.

"Do it again," Frankie said. "Whack them with the hammer."

I belted the side of their van. It dented in like a cannon had hit it.

After that they accelerated. They went up onto the sidewalk. Then they drove back into the street and tried to run us into a parked car. Frankie was an expert driver, though. He knew when to take and when to give.

The road narrowed up ahead into a single lane.

We were almost parallel with them.

"This is it," Frankie said.

All the streetlights turned on simultaneously. They broke my focus on the Pool Universe van. I looked forward and saw a circular hole in the street getting closer. A sewer cover had been pulled off and was sitting next to the hole, about six inches higher than the pavement.

"Frankie," I said. "Watch the sewer!"

Pool Universe hit the manhole cap head on. Their van lurched up and then smashed down against the street. A crack came from their axle and they started to fishtail.

Frankie pulled the e-brake and we dropped back just before they could swerve into us.

Their van slid sideways into the curb, cleared the sidewalk, and went airborne into a retention pond.

They hit the brown water like a plane crashing straight down from the sky. A flock of geese erupted from the splash like squawking fireworks. The dark sky swallowed them almost instantly.

Then everything went silent.

Those two assholes never left their van. It started to go under and the back doors split open. Pool supplies began swimming away from the sinking vehicle.

Frankie stopped the truck.

"Should we help them?" he asked me.

"No. Let them drown."

4

Frankie drove in reverse all the way back to the house.

Then he put the weed pipe and a cigarette in his mouth and lit both together, exhaling the smoke out of his nose like a dragon.

He handed me the pipe and said, "They wanted to play a man's game, but they forgot the only rule."

"What's that?"

"Win."

"You just took them down a road they've only seen in their nightmares. They'll never underestimate a guy called Muscles Marinara again."

"Like my dad always says: 'Sometimes you're the bug, sometimes you're the windshield'."

I took a bowl-clearing hit and thought about our victory. "Dude, I think we're The Peoples' Champions."

"No, Londi. We're The Heavyweight Champions of the World."

"No, Frankie. We're The *World* Heavyweight Champions of the World."

"You're right ... should we hug?"

"No. This ain't over yet."

I got out of the truck and climbed into the bed. I held up the vacuum head and the skimmer net. "Do we vacuum poop, or skim it out?"

Frankie scrapped the residue in the bowl with his keys and tried to find a last hit. "Neither," he coughed. "We're done here."

We walked into the backyard ready for a brawl. Gina and the redhead were at the side of the pool, pointing at the poop. Their bikinis made them look like two starving animals trapped in some roadside petting zoo.

The sliding door opened a few inches and Gina's mom stuck her head out. "Gina, what did I say about that bathing suit? Your father is going to be home any minute."

"The idiots just walked in," Gina said back.

The door slid open so hard it hit the frame and bounced off the track. The mom came running out with a flip flop in her hand. She waved it like she was going to throw it at us and said, "Can you explain to me why I'm still looking at a piece of shit in my pool?"

Frankie pulled off his shirt. He wrapped it around the back of his neck and said, "Sure babes, I'll explain it to you. You're looking at a piece of shit because YOU are a piece of shit."

Her face turned so red you could almost see the aneurysms exploding. She threw the flip flop at Frankie. Instead of ducking away, he let it hit him right between the eyes. Then he smiled at her.

"YOU'RE AN ANIMAL!" She reached inside and grabbed another flip flop. "Get out of my backyard!"

"An animal?" I said. "His blood can be traced back to the Roman Empire, ma'am."

"Oh, big surprise there. God forbid a greaseball leaves southern Italy and *doesn't* end up in New Jersey."

She threw the other flip flop at Frankie, but it missed and landed in the pool.

"Never mind all that about Italy," Frankie said to her. "Fuck Italy. Italy's never done a thing for me. Let me tell you about what I do *here* during pool season. I make every single one of you assholes happy. Fifteen hours a day in plagued water full of death and scum, and I make it beautiful. All your barbecues and your horseshoe tournaments, even that stripper suit your daughter's wearing to give herself skin cancer - that's all because of me. And nobody cares. I get paid $10 an hour to get sun poisoning, bitten by snakes, and handle rotting raccoons so that *you* can live it up. And you know what I get for it? I get people not paying their bills. I get people yelling at me because there's a random piece of shit floating around their pool."

He put his fist into his elbow joint and jerked up his forearm. "So fuck you and fuck your husband."

Then he pivoted, directing his fist at Gina. "And fuck you too. Your mom's right. Go put some goddamn clothes on."

5

I turned the radio on as we drove away. I moved the dial to 1010 WINS for the local news. A police chief finished a press conference and started answering reporters' questions:

"I'd really like the anonymous caller to just come forward," he said. "It isn't often a call leads us to a suspected war criminal."

"How long has he been in the country?" a reporter asked.

"A long time. He probably would've gotten away with his crimes for the rest of his life. Basically, our caller is a real hero. He got a gun off the street *and* solved one of World War II's biggest mysteries."

I changed the station.

"Are you ready to tell me what's going on?" Frankie asked.

"I don't know what you're talking about."

"Good answer. Just deny 'til you die. For everyone's sake."

CHAPTER TWENTY-TWO

1

They say it's your sense of smell that triggers memories most vividly. But I knew it was *the feeling* I'd never forget – not being able to blink or bend because gallons of chlorine had soaked into my pores and melted every drop of moisture. I'd probably never be able to breathe like I used to, either. Too much shock inhaled.

The only way to counter the poison was with domestic cop beer in the morning for clarity, and then a steady intake of harder stuff to maintain. Somehow the Universe provided the medicine to get through this filthy drama just when it was needed most. And as the day wore on, my throat welcomed each gulp like it was water from a mountain spring.

The scars were predominantly mental. But blood flowed from at least three different holes. And my shins had been slashed so many times by the Hayward pump that I might've been permanently hobbled. The possibility of brain damage was also real; tequila and whiskey in the afternoon and weed from 6 a.m. onward does not sustain healthy brain cells. I was pissing straight black from all the coffee, and I was spitting blood from smoking like a broke stove all day.

That clean smell of chlorine might've been the only thing to look back on with a smile.

2

I hated to do it, but I called Lunchbox. The *code* needed to be respected. I was entering his wake.

"Look, Lunchbox," I said, "this might be it for us. But I'm pretty sure I'm making the right choice. I think I love her. And I'm *way* too insecure to keep you in my life."

I expected to hear some platitude like "famous last words," but he said he understood. "Life is about love," he said. "Nothing else should matter."

What a jerk.

3

I had Frankie drop me off at my parents' house. It was time to apologize.

"All right, bro," Frankie said. "I'll pick you up at 5:30 tomorrow?"

"No."

"No?"

"You can't work your way up, Frankie."

"What are you saying?"

"I give up. You should too."

"I'm not going to die poor. Even if it kills me."

"We're too far over the hump. James Dean was our age when he checked out."

A tension released from his face like I had just put into words something he'd always known but never said.

"James Dean was one of the lucky ones. Some people get to write their own legend."

I looked out my passenger window and saw the curtains in my parents' living room shift. The dog's brown head bent to one side, then the other.

As I stepped out of the truck the last chords of a slow song faded from the radio. But the melody lingered, and up in the darkened maple leaves the mockingbirds sang like they had sung every night of my entire life. A tune that I'd never listened to until today. And under that New Jersey spring sky, with long clouds caught somewhere between winter and summer, and the stars constantly fighting to be noticed through New York City's glow, the mockingbirds' hymn would forever remind me of those precious moments of freedom, where I answered to no boss and took no orders.

"It sounds like New Jersey thinks you're a hero," Frankie laughed. "What are you going to do with it?"

A soft rain began to fall around us. Oil dripping from the bottom of the truck slowly swam down the driveway. The truck's headlights illuminated the toxic trickle of water like a bled-out rainbow.

"I'm going to find the Queen," I said. "Maybe she'll want to stare at this disaster with me until the world turns beautiful again."

THE END